CROSSING OVER

A DCI SEAN BRACKEN NOVEL

JOHN CARSON

DCI SEAN BRACKEN SERIES

Starvation Lake

Think Twice

Crossing Over

DCI HARRY MCNEIL SERIES

Return to Evil

Sticks and Stones

Back to Life

Dead Before You Die

Hour of Need

Blood and Tears

Devil to Pay

Point of no Return

Rush to Judgement

Against the Clock

Where Stars Will Shine – a charity anthology
compiled by Emma Mitchell, featuring a
Harry McNeil short story –
The Art of War and Peace

DI FRANK MILLER SERIES

Crash Point

Silent Marker

Rain Town

Watch Me Bleed

Broken Wheels

Sudden Death

Under the Knife

Trial and Error

Warning Sign

Cut Throat

Blood from a Stone

Time of Death

Frank Miller Crime Series – Books 1-3 – Box set

Frank Miller Crime Series - Books 4-6 - Box set

MAX DOYLE SERIES

Final Steps
Code Red
The October Project

SCOTT MARSHALL SERIES

Old Habits

CROSSING OVER

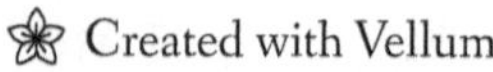 Created with Vellum

To Kit and John. And their families.
Now my family.

ONE

Saturday night

'Who are you?' Meghan asked the man through her blurred eyes.

'Security. Are you okay?' The man was big, with short hair, but that was all she could make out.

'I don't feel too good.'

'Happens every hen night. Usually one of the group who gets blootered, though. This is a first for me, the bride getting well-oiled.'

'I can't find my way back.'

'That's because you're down a private corridor. That's why they sent me to help you.'

'I'm going to be sick,' Meghan said.

'Sit on the floor for a second. Put your head between your legs. Take some deep breaths. Then we'll go and get you a glass of water.'

Meghan slid down the wall onto the floor. She could hear the music from the club filtering downstairs from above. Where her friends were. She sat and put her head down.

'Do you feel any better?' the bouncer asked.

'Not really. My head's swimming. I shouldn't have had those shots so early. Red Bull and vodka.'

'Come on then, let's get you along to one of the private offices. I'll get you some water, then you can have a coffee. I have some aspirin too. Help you feel better.'

She struggled to her feet with the man's help. He held on to her left arm and guided her along the corridor. It had marble floors and little light sconces on the wall, like she was in a fancy hotel.

'Thank you for helping me.' Her legs felt like they were made of rubber and she would have fallen over if it weren't for the big, strong bouncer. She couldn't make out his features; her eyes, filled with tears now, were still blurry. She thought he was familiar, but she couldn't grasp who he was. Maybe if she hadn't had so much to drink.

'Are you...married?' she asked, not sure why she was asking.

He ignored her as they turned a corner and he stopped at a door.

'Here, this is an office. You sit in here. If the management knew you were down here, they'd call the police. But you just need some water and a coffee.'

He opened the door and ushered her gently inside, guiding her round the desk and getting her to sit at it. The big leather chair made a squishing noise as she dropped into it.

'Don't go away. I'll get you a bottle of water from the fridge.'

She didn't ask where the fridge was. Or where he would get her a coffee, but both would be good right now.

He left the door open and she could hear his shoes clacking on the marble floor. The music from the night-club above lightly filtered through to her.

She felt her insides churning, and her lower gut was on fire. Maybe she should try to find a toilet again. She tried to get up out of the chair but didn't have enough strength. Hopefully, she could hold on until her friend returned.

She was beginning to think he wasn't coming back when the door opened again and in he walked. Her tall, dark stranger.

'Water?' she asked, not quite seeing what he had in his hands.

'I've got something better than water,' he said, closing the door behind him.

TWO

Earlier that day

'Aye, nothing a wee bit of Polyfilla and a couple of nails won't fix,' Detective Chief Inspector Sean Bracken said to his boss.

Detective Superintendent Kara Page managed a wry smile as she looked at the burnt-out remains of what was once her house. A chill wind whipped across the fields behind and stirred the snow that still lay on the ground.

'A lick of paint and she'll be as good as new.'

'That's the spirit.'

She turned to Bracken. 'Nothing yet?'

He dug his hands deeper into the pockets of his coat. Shook his head. 'Nothing yet,' he confirmed. It was the same question she kept asking and he couldn't blame her. It was twinned with, *And you're sure you heard him correctly?* Words that a killer had spoken to Bracken, denying he was responsible for burning the house.

They were looking for the owner of an old green Land Rover last seen exiting the back drive of Kara's house, the main suspect in the arson job. They thought they'd caught him when they caught the killer they were hunting two weeks ago, but just before he died that man had denied burning down Kara's house.

There was no reason for Bracken to suspect he was lying. This man had been an egomaniac and would have loved to have taken the credit for it, but only if he had set the fire.

'Edwin Hawk and Stella Graham didn't waste any time getting married,' she said, her nose and cheeks rosy with the cold.

Hawk was an American writer and psychologist who had been a suspect in their last case but had turned out to be innocent.

'Good luck to him. He deserves a little bit of happiness.'

'We all do, Sean.'

'You going back down the road?' he asked her.

Kara shook her head. 'I'm going to do some shopping. Not food shopping, obviously, but I'm going to treat myself. Something decadent that I don't need but want. Then I'm having dinner with an old friend.'

'Sounds good to me.'

'You going home?'

'Yes, I'll head on down. I'm going to see my daughter this evening. It's late Saturday afternoon so she'll probably just be getting out of bed. You know what students are like.'

Home for both Bracken and Kara was a guest house in Corstorphine, owned and run by Bracken's old friend and ex-colleague Bob Long and his wife, Mary. They had invested their money in the house after Bob was medically pensioned out of the force having broken his back trying to save two kids.

'I have to make a decision soon,' Kara said as he was about to turn away. 'About whether I want to have this place pulled down and rebuilt or have them repair it.'

'If it was me, I'd demolish it and all the bad memories that go with it. Rebuild, then sell it.'

'Sell it? You think that's the better way to go?'

He nodded past the wreck of her house. 'You have a huge back garden. There are fields on the other side of the road, a few houses either side of you. I don't see anybody coming round with a home-baked apple pie to offer you something to eat or words of wisdom.'

'This isn't a Henry Fonda film.'

'You know what I mean. Do you even know your

next-door neighbour's name? And I use the term loosely since he lives across the other side of the road that runs next to your house.'

Kara shuddered for a moment as if somebody had walked across her future grave. 'Ken something.'

'Ken? With his wife, Barbie?'

She made a face.

'It's all about quality of life,' Bracken said. 'I know I'm one to talk; I live in the guest house.'

'I do too. Don't make it sound like the murder mansion.'

'You have a chance to get this place made like new and the market is hot right now. You'll sell it, no problem. To somebody who will invite Ken and Barbie round for a barbeque. Or a wee drive in their beach buggy.' He smiled at her.

'You always know the right things to say,' she replied, smiling.

'Then when you have the proceeds from this place, you can buy somewhere nice. Where the neighbours are real and will take an interest in you. Like any decent neighbour should.'

'I'll probably do that. Thanks for coming up here on your day off and giving me your opinion.'

'Anytime,' Bracken said.

'What about your dad?'

Bracken's father, Ed, was in the same predicament as Kara: his home had burnt down. But his house was a double-wide mobile home, which wasn't technically a mobile home because it couldn't be moved. The old man had explained things to Bracken one night when they'd had a quiet drink in the lounge of the guest house. Ed Bracken was staying there too, with his German shepherd, Max.

'He said it's going to be a wee while as his insurance payout was a bit short. He'll get a new one soon.' *Please God.*

Kara smiled. 'I like your dad. He's a good laugh. I can tell you're best friends.'

'Aye, well, that's not quite how I would put it, but he's alright.'

'When he was being held and you thought he was going to die, you raced after him and saved his life. That's what I would call being best friends.'

'You've not got many friends, have you, ma'am? All due respect.'

She laughed. 'I had one or two, a long time ago. And I just told you I'm having dinner with one.' She looked at the house before looking at him. 'Let's not forget you ran into that house there to save me too. I owe you a debt of gratitude.'

'I'm sure Ken would have rushed over in his VW microbus and saved you too.'

She laughed and nudged his arm. 'You ever get lonely, Sean?'

'I do. Chaz and I go out for a drink now and again, and I go over to her place to play some board games or watch a film, but...I don't know. It's like there's something missing.' He looked at her. 'How about you?'

She nodded. 'I love the guest house, but I never forget it's somebody else's house, no matter how nice it is.' She took her eyes off the charred wood and looked at him again. 'I don't know how I'm ever going to repay you for doing what you did.'

'You and my dad can keep each other company. Keep him out of my hair. Debt paid in full.'

'We play poker and have a couple of drinks. We're not planning on going on a cruise together.'

'This decadent thing you're planning on buying? Edible or wearable?'

'Not sure. Why?'

'You wear a ladies' Omega watch. Go for a subtle pair of earrings. And a nice box of chocolates. But whatever you do, don't bet your earrings when you play poker with my dad again.'

THREE

'You still seeing Sarah tonight?' Ed Bracken asked his son. They were sitting in the lounge of the guest house. Max lay by the gas fire, hogging the heat.

'Aye. We're having a wee drink.' Bracken didn't tell his dad he was worried about his daughter. It would only get the old man rambling on about how things were 'taken care of' in the old days. Yet he'd never seen his dad get into a fight in his life.

'Tell her that her grandpa needs a wee visit.'

'So you can wipe her out at poker? Aye, I'll pass that message on.'

'How dare you. That's my grandchild. You, on the other hand, I would take to the cleaner's.'

'I'll have that put on my tombstone: "Here lies Sean Bracken. Taken to the cleaner's."'

'I wish you wouldn't talk like that.'

'Relax. I don't plan on popping off any time soon.'

'Nobody does, son. Some people don't get a choice, though, eh?'

They sat in silence for a moment. The TV was on, but it was muted.

'Anyway, that killed the conversation,' Bracken said.

'Right, I need your help with something,' Ed said.

'Putting the fire out?'

'What fire?'

'Max. Dad, his fur's smoking.'

'He's fine.'

'Will he lie there until he spontaneously combusts or something?'

'He likes the heat. He'll get up when he's too hot. But anyway, pay attention. I need your help with my dancing.'

'What do you mean, your dancing?' Bracken said, looking suspiciously at his father.

'I'm going to a do tonight. At the Watsonians'. Right proper do it is too. Peter Fisher is having a party. Celebrating his daughter, Meghan, getting married.'

'Peter Fisher? The finance guy?'

'The very same. It's his daughter's hen night tonight, and his future son-in-law is having a stag do in Dublin.'

'And you're invited along? I mean, as a guest, not as a waiter?'

'Don't be bloody funny now. Peter and I go way back. He's a great guy.'

Bracken wondered at what point in life his father and Peter Fisher had reached a fork in the road and gone down different paths. Obviously, Fisher had taken the road less travelled, while Ed Bracken had sweated in an office all his life.

'Why are they getting married in January? Why not June?' Bracken asked.

'They're getting married next month. Who am I to ask why they have to get married?' Ed replied, silently insinuating that there might not have been a choice, to spare the family some blushes. 'Besides, they're just having their last fling here for their pals. The wedding is taking place in Barbados. I don't think it's snowing down there, but please feel free to correct me if I'm wrong.'

'Okay, point taken. Now, what about this dancing lark? I'd have thought you'd have been an expert years before I was born. The reason I *was* born. Meeting my mother at the dancing.'

'Here, enough of that talk.'

'I'm surprised I wasn't one of the altar boys at your wedding,' Bracken said.

'Do you want to help me or not?'

'Of course. What do you want me to do?'

'Dance with me.'

Bracken looked at his father. 'I'm waiting for the punchline.'

'There's no punchline. I just need to practise a wee bit of dancing. I haven't had a dance since your mother passed away. I'm a wee bit rusty.'

'If you're taking the piss...' Bracken said.

Ed held up his hands. Max looked up to see what was going on, then flopped his head back down again. 'I'm not. Help a brother out.'

'Well...*Dad*...I'm all for helping somebody, but this is above and beyond.'

'Aw, come on. Remember all those times I sat with you while you were studying for the police exam? Helping you with your arithmetic because if any answer went above ten, you'd have to take your shoes off to carry on adding with your toes?'

'You're hilarious.'

'But I did help you. And you sailed through the exam.'

'Oh, God. Emotional blackmail this is called,' Bracken said, relenting. 'Okay, but twice round the dancefloor, and don't forget where you are. None of this having a blackout and asking me up to your room.'

'Bloody behave yourself.'

'What about music?' Bracken asked.

'I've got one of those wee Bluetooth speakers. There are foxtrot mixes on YouTube. I'll play one.'

'You've come prepared. But let me ask you: why didn't you ask Mary?'

'She's out today.'

'You could have waited until she came home.'

'I have to take a shower.'

'Why? The summer solstice isn't even close,' Bracken said.

'Come on, for God's sake,' Ed said, shaking his head.

'You owe me one for this.'

'Aye, aye, come on. Let's get started.' Max didn't budge as Ed fiddled with his phone. 'Bloody thing.'

'Let me try.'

'I'll get it. I'm not bloody senile.'

Bracken thought that his father was either going to connect the speaker or inadvertently hack into the National Grid and cause a power cut.

Then music came through the speaker and no lights went out, Bracken was glad to see.

'Right, I'll be the man, obviously,' Ed said, holding his hands out, 'and you can be the woman.'

'Christ, I knew there would be a catch. Why can't I be the man? I'm taller than you.'

'I might be dancing with a taller woman. But just concentrate. Let the music take us away.'

'Aye, so I will.'

'Come on, stop messing about.'

'Don't be grabbing my arse. There's only so much role play I can take.'

'Shut up.'

At that moment, Bob Long came along the corridor from the back of the house, carrying a tray with a coffee pot and cups on it. He nudged the door with his foot.

'No, you put your hands the other way,' Ed said.

'Listen, I know what I'm doing. I'm a woman now,' Bracken said.

Bob dropped the tray of cups onto the floor with a crash.

'Christ,' he said as the lid fired off, spilling coffee on the carpet.

'You okay there?' Ed said as Max jumped to his feet and started barking. He silenced the music.

'Er, I...sorry. It just slipped out of my hands,' Bob said, looking at Bracken. 'Sorry, I didn't realise...'

'Hush now,' Ed said to the dog. Max quietened down.

'Realise what?' Bracken said.

'You know.' Bob nodded to him. 'You know...that you were...'

'What?' Bracken said.

'Are you going to make me say it? A bloody

woman. I mean, there's nothing wrong with it, but you could have mentioned it. Is that why you got divorced?'

Bracken looked puzzled for a second. 'No, I'm just helping my dad –'

'Practise self-defence,' Ed said, jumping in.

'Oh, right. Jesus. And you were pretending to be a female victim?' Bob looked at his friend.

'Aye, that's it,' Bracken confirmed.

'Right. As I said, nothing wrong with it. I just didn't see you as a woman. I'll get a cloth and brush,' Bob said, scuttling away.

'Are you daft?' Ed asked his son. 'You were going to tell him we were dancing.'

'We were, remember?'

'Aye, but Bob doesn't have to know that.'

'He was bringing coffee.'

'I hadn't asked him to,' Ed said.

'Right, you're on your own from now on, old man. I hope the woman you dance with doesn't have two left feet.'

They all mucked in clearing up the china, which miraculously hadn't broken when it landed on the carpet.

'What are you doing tonight?' Bob asked Bracken.

'Whatever it is, it won't be dancing.'

FOUR

'Are you sure Sarah won't mind me coming along?' Chaz Cullen said as they stood at the bus stop, snow falling again.

Bracken looked out of the shelter, wondering if he should spring for a taxi, but there were none with their yellow lights on. His wallet lived to see another day.

'She said she's fine with it. I told her I was bringing a friend along. I mean, it's not as if she was shy about bringing *her* friend along last time.'

'The friend you want to talk to her about?'

Bracken looked at her. 'I'm just going to ask if she's seen him again since he dumped her.'

'Do you think I look alright?' Chaz looked herself up and down; black overcoat, black jeans and boots.

'Well, you're hardly the Bride of Frankenstein.'

'That's not quite what I was fishing for, but from you, I take it as a compliment.'

'I meant you look fine. It's winter. I don't think she'll be expecting you to turn up in a mini skirt.'

'I don't own a mini skirt.'

'There you go then.' He looked at her closely. 'The blue streak in your hair isn't so noticeable anymore.'

'I'm toning it down a bit.'

'I thought you were practising for having a blue rinse one day.'

'In thirty years' time, I'll revisit the idea,' she replied. 'Meantime, I'll stick to natural brunette.'

He could see the bus trundling along in the distance, coming along Glasgow Road from the Gogar end.

'You seem a bit grumpy tonight. Everything okay?'

He looked at her. They were friends, good friends at that, and sometimes he thought she could read him better than he could read himself.

My dad and I were dancing in the lounge and Bob walked in and caught us. He shuddered at how that would sound if he said it out loud. 'Sorry. I know we were planning on pizza and a movie at yours, but this thing with Mark Turner is doing my heid in now.'

'You're doing the right thing. We can do pizza any night.'

He looked at her and smiled. 'Aye.'

The guest house was on the main road in Corstorphine, near Edinburgh Zoo, and it was only a five-minute walk to Chaz's flat. He had never stayed the night, but he'd only been seeing her for a few weeks. Not even seeing her, in the traditional sense. *Hanging out with her* seemed a trifle too much like what a teenager would do, but that was the essence of it. It was how he had described his relationship with her when his nosey father had started questioning him like he was fifteen again.

'Will she move back in with Catherine?' Chaz asked, shrugging herself deeper into her overcoat.

Catherine Bracken, his ex-wife and Sarah's mother.

'I know Sarah is going to Edinburgh Uni and her mother also lives in Edinburgh, but right now Sarah wants to do the student thing. I used to think that involved living in a flat with some other layabouts, but apparently it also involves drinking copious amounts of alcohol and skipping out on some classes when dealing with a hangover which takes precedence over learning.'

'I was like that too. Many moons ago.'

The bus sloshed into the side of the road and they got on. It was starting to fill up the closer to town it got. They chatted until they got into town, Chaz asking him if he had downloaded Spotify yet.

'Not yet. My CD collection gets me through.'

She laughed. 'Even Ed has Spotify. What, you drag out your old CD player when you feel like listening to a Queen album?'

'Nothing wrong with Queen. The old stuff. *A Day at the Races.*'

'They have Queen on Spotify.'

'You're like a broken record. If you'll pardon the pun.' He nudged her in the ribs and smiled at her. Truth was, he felt like he was getting old at times. Forty-five going on sixty-five. He remembered the good times with his wife, when they had gone out as a foursome with Bob and Mary.

'Come on, this is our stop,' Chaz said as the bus pulled into the side of the road in Princes Street, close to Frederick Street.

They trudged through the snow uphill towards George Street.

'Don't worry, it's all downhill from here,' Chaz said, and he wasn't sure if she meant it literally or was referring to the state of their friendship.

The pub was near Jamaica Street. Barney McGroo's. He wondered if the owner had been a fan of *Trumpton.*

'God knows where they get the names from,' he said, and the bouncer nodded at him. Bracken made eye contact with the young man. He knew him from way back, had given him a break one night. The man would have his back if something kicked off.

'Good to see you again, sir,' the bouncer said, reaching for the door handle.

'You too, son.'

And that was the length of their interaction.

'Friends in low places?' Chaz said, a slight smile on her face.

'I've got friends everywhere.' Bracken spotted Sarah sitting at a table with a young man he didn't recognise. He made the internationally recognised hand signal, asking if she wanted a drink. Sarah smiled and gave him a thumbs-up. *The usual.*

Christ, his little girl had a *usual.* The wee girl who used to play with dolls and watch cartoons was now drinking alcohol.

'I'm going to the ladies,' Chaz said.

'Okay, I'll get your usual?' It didn't seem too bad when his friend had a *usual.* That, he could live with.

'Please.'

Bracken got the drinks. The place was busy but not *we're all going to die if there's a fire* overcrowded. He took the drinks over to the table and placed them down.

'Sorry, pal, we're having a conversation here,' the young man said, standing up to his full height. Not quite as big as Bracken, but close.

'Don't let me stop you, son.'

'Excuse me?' He looked as if Bracken had said he smelled like shit.

'Do you know him?' Bracken asked Sarah.

'No, we were just chatting.'

'Aye, so if you don't mind...' the man started to say, poking his finger at Bracken's chest.

'Son, if that finger touches me, I'll not only break it, but I'll break you into a thousand pieces.'

'Is that fucking right?'

Bracken didn't really want to bring his warrant card into play, but knew it might be the better option. 'Aye, that is fucking right. I'm polis, and if I have to break you, I'll also arrest you for assaulting a police officer. Next move is yours.'

The man didn't look so sure of himself now. 'Want her for yourself, do you?'

'She's my fucking daughter, so if I were you, I would think very carefully about the next words out of your mouth. They might be the last ones for a long time until you learn how to speak again.'

Sarah looked at the young man and smiled, nodding her head.

He walked away, mumbling, and Bracken sat down next to his daughter, his back to the wall, with an eye on the door.

'In the door five minutes and already you're threatening to knock somebody out,' Sarah said. 'That's a record.'

'Hey, he started it.'

'My daddy, the big protector.' She gave a laugh and accepted the drink. 'Where's your friend? Or is she just an imaginary one?'

'See for yourself.' He nodded to Chaz, who was coming over. She had taken her overcoat off, and Bracken saw she had a sweater on, but not like the one she had worn at Christmas.

'Chaz, this is Sarah.'

She reached over and shook Sarah's hand. 'Your dad and I work together.'

'I know. He's told me all about you,' Sarah said as Chaz sat down.

'Nice things, I hope?'

Sarah held her hand out and wiggled it about. Then she laughed. 'Of course.'

Bracken took a sip of his drink. 'I have a message from your grandpa: he needs a visit.'

Sarah's face fell. 'Is something wrong?'

'No, no, nothing like that. He just wants to see his wee granddaughter.'

'I know. I haven't seen him for a wee while. I'll visit him this week before we go back to uni. We can take Max to the park.'

'He'll like that.' He took another sip of his drink.

'You work in the pathology place, my dad says,' Sarah said to Chaz.

'Pathology place?' Bracken said. 'You're doing a business degree. It's called a mortuary.'

Sarah laughed. 'I couldn't think of the word for a minute. Sorry, Chaz.'

'It's okay. But yes, I'm an assistant there.'

'I couldn't do that. Or my dad's job. I think I would puke at the sight of the dead people. Oh, God. I admire you for doing that sort of job.'

'Believe it or not, you get used to it.'

They sat in silence for a moment. 'What is it you wanted to see me about, Dad?'

'Have you seen Mark Turner again?'

Sarah shook her head. 'No, I haven't seen him since he dumped me before New Year's. I think he didn't like the fact you're a big, bad copper.'

'I want you to let me know if he gets in contact with you again.'

'Why?'

'He's bad news, Sarah.'

'You checked up on him, didn't you? Did you talk to him behind my back?'

'No, nothing like that,' Bracken said, trying to reassure his daughter. 'Well, maybe a wee bit. He hangs out with some rough people.'

'He's nice, though. He was always a gentleman.'

Bracken looked at his pint glass for a second, hoping what he was about to say would sound the same out loud as it had done in his head when he was practising.

His father was a bank robber. Billy Turner. He's dead now. I shot the bastard. No, those words wouldn't come out right no matter how hard he tried.

'All I'm saying is, be careful. He's not good news.'

Sarah looked annoyed for a moment. 'I'm sure I would have got to know Mark a lot better if we had started dating.' She looked at Chaz. 'We were about to, until my dad put the kibosh on it. I liked him a lot, but then he ghosted me. Dumped by my boyfriend before he became my boyfriend. I was that close.' She held her thumb and index finger close together.

'Just be careful.'

Sarah sipped her drink. 'I'm not sure what's going on with Mark then. Does he know you?'

'I'm assuming he does. I don't know why, but he was getting close to you. Now, it might be a coincidence, but...'

'Coppers don't believe in coincidence. Blah blah blah. I've seen all the TV shows, Dad.'

'I just want you to be careful. If he shows up again, you call me, okay?'

'I just had a few drinks with him. He hung out with us.'

'What about his friends?'

'He was always on his own.'

'Just promise me, Sarah. You'll call me if he ever comes into your company again. He isn't who he seems to be.'

'Okay. I promise.'

They had a few more drinks before Sarah said she was meeting a friend in a few minutes. Then a young couple walked in and she introduced them. 'Lindsay, this is my dad and his friend, Chaz.'

They shook hands. Lindsay introduced her boyfriend. 'This is Adam Malone.'

'Hello, folks. Buy you a drink?'

'You're fine, son, thanks anyway. We were just leaving.'

'If you're sure.'

'Absolutely, Adam.'

They all left together. Bracken was the last one out, and he caught movement out of the corner of his eye as he watched his surroundings. The concrete pathway to the front door had been shovelled but was being covered with snow again.

A man was coming up fast behind him. Bracken thought it was the man from inside the pub and turned round to deal with him, but the bouncer had stuck a boot out and tripped the man.

'Oh, ya bastard,' the man said, landing on his face.

Bracken looked at the bouncer and gave him a quick salute. The bouncer nodded back.

This time, Bracken flagged down a taxi.

FIVE

'I'm not holding you back, am I?' Bracken said to Chaz as they got out of the taxi at the guest house.

'What do you mean?' The snow had stopped, but a bitter wind hit them.

'Christ, look at me; the highlight of my week is having a couple of drinks with my daughter before she scoots off to be with her uni mates. Come back home and it's barely gone ten.'

'Don't be daft. I enjoy spending time with you.'

'Aye, but I'm forty-five and you're thirty-two. You could be up the town at one of those places where they play old music for young lassies like you to get yourself a sugar daddy. Or nightclubs where you can't hear what the other person is saying because your ears are bleeding.'

'I only hang about with you out of pity. I mean, I don't want you to slip and break a hip.'

'Aye, that would ruin my chances at the Disco-Dancing World Championships right enough.'

'Listen to you; disco. What's that? I'll have to Google it.'

'Bloody cheek. But proves my point.'

He wondered if this was why he hadn't spent the night with her. Deep down, he felt he was too old for her, the thirteen-year age gap more than just a number in his head.

'Come on, dafty, let's go in and get Max from Bob and Mary. We can take him for a wee walk, then we can take him back to my place.' She smiled at him. 'If I didn't want to be around you, Sean Bracken, I would say so.'

'Aye, a wee walk then up for a coffee sounds just the ticket,' he said.

They went into the guest house, where they could hear Max barking through the back.

'Protective wee bugger, isn't he?' Bracken said. 'I hope he hasn't woken old Mr and Mrs Clark.'

'I'm sure they're out for the count,' Chaz said.

They saw a light on in the lounge through the glass-panelled door. Bracken saw Kara sitting with Natalie Hogan, Bob and Mary's niece and a permanent resident. She was looking after her eight-year-old son. She had lost custody of Rory but was helping out her ex-husband at the moment.

Chaz waved at them and they brightened up when they saw her.

'Go and get Max and I'll sit with the girls,' Chaz said to Bracken. She went into the lounge. 'Hello, ladies. How are you tonight?'

'We were just talking about having a girls' night out soon,' Natalie said. 'You'd be up for that, wouldn't you?'

'Of course I would. A meal and some drinks?'

'Absolutely,' Kara said.

'If you can drag yourself away from your boyfriend,' Natalie said, grinning.

'We're just friends, Nat,' Chaz said, her face burning from the heat now.

'Of course you are.'

They heard voices from the back and the sound of Bracken returning.

'Here he is, the wild animal,' Natalie said. 'And Max too.'

'You're all funny, you know that?' Bracken said as Max strained on the leash.

'Hey, baby,' Natalie said, and the dog rushed over to nuzzle her as she sat on a chair.

'You're home early,' Kara said, looking at Bracken.

'We're just here to pick up Max and we're going to

Chaz's place.' He saw the earrings she was wearing. 'Nice choice.'

She put a hand up to one ear. 'They were my grandmother's. I bought a couple of books.'

'That's what I meant. The latest Clive Cussler.'

She looked quickly at the book that was sitting on the small table next to the couch.

'They should pay *you* the big bucks, Detective.' She smiled at him as he took the dog away from Natalie, whom Max seemed to be bonding with more and more.

'Give me a call about the night out?' Chaz said to Kara.

'You bet.'

They left with the dog, who stopped on the snow covering the small car park at the front of the house. Max loved to pee everywhere, but this was the dog's preferred spot.

'Good boy. Let's go and see Auntie Chaz's place. Maybe she'll have some whisky in. Let's ask her, shall we?' He looked at Chaz. 'Dog wants to know if you have whisky in.'

'Tell him no. But I have some beer.'

Max tilted his head at her as they walked down the short drive to the pavement. 'He says that'll do.'

'Do I get brownie points if it's cold and in bottles?'

Bracken looked at her. 'He says you do.'

'Then let's go get some. They're in my fridge.'

'I wonder how my dad's getting on?'

'You make it sound like it was an interview he was going to.'

'He was a bit nervous about his rusty dancing skills. I gave him some pointers.' Like, *if you tell anybody we were doing the foxtrot in Bob's lounge, I'll put you in a home.*

'I'm sure he'll appreciate that.'

'You don't know how true that is.'

SIX

Bracken fixed his tie and looked in the mirror of the en-suite bathroom. Then he took his mobile phone out of his pocket and let his thumb hover over the screen. Was it too early to call Catherine? It was Monday morning, so his ex-wife would be getting ready for her job at the bank; he wouldn't be waking her up.

So why was he hesitating?

He was standing on the ledge, figuratively. He didn't want to leap until he was sure. He put the phone away and walked back into his room. Outside his window, the traffic was slowly heading into Edinburgh city centre, battling the snow. Like he would be doing after breakfast.

He went downstairs and found old Mr and Mrs Clark in the dining room.

'Everything okay with your bank account?' he

asked them, using a quiet voice even though there was nobody else in the room yet.

'Yes, thanks, Sean,' Mrs Clark said.

Bracken had intervened when their son had wiped them out financially, making sure the young man saw the error of his ways and that the couple got their money back. He wanted to make sure that everything was still running smoothly.

'It's all there, son,' Mr Clark said. 'Thanks to you.'

'Thanks to Santa Claus, remember?' Bracken said, smiling at them.

They both laughed.

'Isn't Ed coming down to breakfast this morning?' Mrs Clark asked.

'I thought he would be down here already.' Bracken was puzzled; his old man had been walking on egg shells yesterday after Saturday night's party, complaining that his head was about to explode, and had briefly toyed with the idea of giving up drink forever.

Then they heard the front door open and close, and Bracken looked out into the hallway to see his dad with Max, shaking snow off his jacket.

'Thought I'd get along for the paper,' he said. 'Max was needing to go out too. How're you this morning, son?'

'Fighting fit, of course. I thought you would still be nursing a hangover.'

'Who has a hangover two days in a row? Nah, I was raring to go this morning.'

'Hence the jog to the newsagent's.' Bracken petted the dog as he shot over to him after shaking snow everywhere from his fur.

'How're you feeling this morning?'

'Same as every morning, Dad.'

'You look like a string vest that's been through the wringer too many times.'

'You missed your calling in life.'

'Oh, aye? What's that, son?'

'Being a doctor. Or a clown. I'm going out on a limb, but I think you should have run away to the circus.'

'You're too funny. But give me my dog back. We both need breakfast.'

'Is the room still working out for you?' Bracken asked.

'Aye. It's smaller than the regular room, but it still has its own wee bathroom, so I'm fine. It was good of Bob and Mary to let me use it. God knows when I'll have the extra cash for the new unit.'

'Look, I can help you, Dad.'

Ed put up a hand. 'You have enough on your plate.

You have to find your own place. And I'm not hinting about coming to live with you.'

'Just give me a shout if you need a loan.'

'Despite what people say about you, you're a good lad.'

'What do people say?' Bracken asked, but his father was heading upstairs, laughing, the dog running in front.

Later on, when Bracken was having another coffee before heading off to work, Kara Page came into the lounge, where he was watching the morning news.

'I just got a call,' she said. 'I can come in your car.'

'Where are we going?'

'Clubbing,' she said. 'Blues and twos. We don't want to keep the others waiting.'

SEVEN

The Vaults was a club at the east end of George Street. Once a bank, the building was a restaurant-bar with the nightclub downstairs. That end of the street was blocked off with patrol cars, Bracken found, as he guided his car around one of the parked vehicles, his siren off but the blues still doing their thing.

'Edinburgh was your haunt years ago, Sean,' Kara said. 'This place any good?'

'I've never been here before, ma'am. I was more of a spit and sawdust sort of man. I was never one for putting gel in my hair and not shaving for a few days to try and attract women.'

'You were married, though. You didn't have to.'

He pulled the car into the side of the road behind some more patrol cars and an ambulance.

'Doesn't mean I didn't stop trying. Catherine had a little, what shall we call it, dalliance?'

'Ah.'

'What about you? This your sort of place?'

'I spent Saturday night in the guest house lounge, having a couple of beers with Natalie. You figure it out.'

They stepped into the cold morning air. The snow was still deciding whether it wanted to have a pagger with Edinburgh. Bracken slipped as he got onto the pavement and thought the weather was winning. He remembered what Chaz had said about him falling and breaking a hip.

Young people fall and break a hip, he should have said to her, but it was too late now.

There were uniforms standing near an arched gateway along from the stone steps that led up to the main entrance. Bracken and Kara showed their warrant cards.

'Checkers nightclub,' Bracken said. He looked at Kara. 'I met Sarah in a pub called Barney McGroo's on Saturday night. Do you think there's a committee who sit late into the night, trying to think up the strangest names for pubs and clubs?'

'Probably. If I ever buy a pub, it's going to be called Kara's. Pure and simple.'

He'd thought she was going to say *The Pig and Whistle* for a moment.

A door at the side was open. Down the hallway was a staircase that led down to the vaults of the old bank.

Detective Inspector Jimmy Sullivan was at the bottom. He was wearing nitrile gloves, as if expecting to give his two superior officers a rectal exam before allowing them in.

'Morning, ma'am. Sir,' he said.

'I was only given a brief rundown on the phone, Inspector,' Kara said. 'What are the details?'

'Down this way. There's another set of stairs that lead down to the offices through these doors.'

They passed the main doors that led into the club and went through a double set of doors that had been jammed open.

'The deceased is a young female,' Sullivan said, his voice bouncing off the ornate walls and steps. Looked like they were made of marble to Bracken's untrained eye. Maybe his ex-wife would be able to tell, since she worked in one of the few remaining bank branches that hadn't been turned into a den of iniquity.

They reached the bottom. Another door, leading to offices. It looked like the lobby of some expensive hotel. The doors all had glass top halves.

'It's the office round the corner along here,'

Sullivan said, in case Bracken and Kara had missed the group of people hovering around there.

They made their way past the uniforms and found Detective Sergeant Ishita Khan there.

'Morning, Izzie,' Bracken said.

'Good morning, sir.'

'Where is she?'

'In there.'

There were several offices in this hallway. Bracken looked into the office where things seemed to be happening. There wasn't room for them all, so those who weren't needed at that second were relegated to the cheap seats.

'Why were MIT called?' Kara asked.

'CID were called in by uniforms, but there was a note on the desk. Looks like a suicide note, but no signature. So they passed the buck.'

'Fair enough.'

Inside, Dr Pamela Green was dressed in a white disposable suit, which definitely would have looked out of place with the night clubbers if the deceased was anything to go by.

'Ah, good morning, detectives,' she said.

Chaz was also dressed in a white suit and smiled when she saw Bracken.

'Good morning,' Bracken answered, and Kara followed suit.

'First impressions, Doctor?' Kara said.

'There's an empty vodka bottle on the floor by the desk. Depends on how much she had to drink before that, but if she drank the whole bottle, it might have been enough to cause alcohol poisoning. But it's all relevant; not just body weight and things like that but her tolerance to alcohol. We'll know a lot more when we get the tox screen done.'

Bracken was looking at the young woman slumped in the leather office chair. Vomit had run out of her mouth and down her left cheek. Her hair looked messed up, like she had tried to comb it with her fingers and done a bad job.

She was wearing a sophisticated-looking white dress. There was an expensive-looking watch on the wrist of her left arm, which was resting in her lap. He looked closer and saw it was a Cartier.

He turned to the note on the desk in front of her. It was sitting on a blotter. There was a little desk organiser off to one side. A telephone sat on the other side.

He read it out loud to Kara.

'I'm sorry. I couldn't go through with the marriage. It was a lie. I'm seeing somebody else, but I know I can't be with him. So I'm taking the easy way out. Love you, Mum.

Meghan.'

Bracken looked up from the piece of paper at his boss. 'Handwritten. Her name's written, not signed.'

Kara looked at him, then down towards the note. 'We've seen it before, a murder made to look like a suicide. Let's get it to the lab and have it checked for prints.'

Bracken suddenly looked at the young woman, at her dead face, and felt a stab of something. Normally, he was detached at a crime scene. It was the only way to make it through the day. But now, he felt like a parent who'd just been told their child was dead.

His father's words came back to him from Saturday night, about going to the party of his friend, Peter Fisher. *Celebrating his daughter, Meghan, getting married,* he had said.

EIGHT

Bracken looked at Izzie. 'Was there any ID on her?'

'Yes, sir. A driving licence. Meghan Fisher. Aged twenty-seven.'

Then Bracken felt his stomach drop like he was in a lift that was being sucked towards ground level with no cables attached.

'Is there a phone?'

'No, we couldn't find one. Her purse is still there, where we found the licence, and there's a fair bit of cash in it.'

'Anybody do a search for next of kin?'

'Not yet. We've been processing the scene.'

He asked for the address and Izzie pulled her notebook out and read it off.

Bracken thought he'd have to call his dad in a little while.

'What's your estimate on time of death?' he asked Dr Green.

'I was telling Chaz that I think it was around midnight Saturday night. Give or take.'

'Thanks.'

Just then, a ginger-haired young woman poked her head round the corner of the doorway. DC Elsie McDade. Their previous recruit had been ready to join the team but had decided his way forward with Police Scotland was with drugs. Not on the drug squad but smoking weed at a party. When Bracken and Kara had discussed the man's future with MIT Edinburgh, Kara had told him that Brogan's arse 'was out the window'. Luckily, she knew an up-and-coming young detective in Inverness who fitted the bill and who was also on the waiting list for MIT. A swift telephone call and an offer to transfer to Edinburgh followed, and the young woman jumped at the chance.

'The manager's just arrived, sir,' said Elsie. 'He's throwing a fit about all the police in his club.'

'Good,' Bracken said. 'I'll have a talk with him. Where is he right now?'

'Upstairs. He said he'll be in his office.'

'So he wants to talk? That's good.'

'That's not exactly what he said. He mentioned ripping you a new body part.'

'Did he now. Well, I'd better not disappoint him. I

should at least go and give him the opportunity. Izzie? Make sure there's an ambulance on standby. I've had my Weetabix this morning and I'm feeling like there might be a bit of verbal sparring going on by the looks of things. Jimmy? With me.'

Izzie gave them the manager's name before Bracken and Sullivan left.

They went back up the shiny marble stairs and Bracken didn't want to be the one to ask if there was a lift in the building.

'There's a wee lift at the end of the corridor where the offices are,' Sullivan said as if reading his mind. They walked along a hallway behind the bar, out of sight of the main drinking hall.

'No need for a lift,' Bracken said, pretending that he couldn't feel the line of sweat along his brow. 'Is there?'

'Not for me.'

'Just for me then?' Bracken said as they started on what felt like the next leg of their attempt to reach the summit of Everest. 'Cheeky bastard.'

'I'm not saying you're not fit, sir. Obviously, I can hardly keep up with you.'

Bracken looked to see if Sullivan was taking the piss, but he had his resting bitch face on. Truth was, Bracken's doctor had told him to ease up on his sugar intake.

'*Sean, your A1C level is pretty high. I'm not saying it's deadly just yet, but if you were a horse, I'd shoot you.*'

Despite cutting back on his favourite three Cs – chocolate chip cookies – he wasn't noticing a drastic reduction in his waistline.

'That Mackenzie Brogan must have been a right cocky wee bastard,' Bracken said as they walked along to an office area. There was a uniform standing outside a door that was wide open. *Easier to hear you shouting, Grandma.*

'I reckon so. I can't imagine throwing my chances away like that.'

'No, you just like to take the piss out of a senior officer.'

The uniform acknowledged them and Bracken knocked on the open door.

'What?' a man yelled from inside.

'DCI Bracken. DI Sullivan. Mr Flynn?'

'Yes. Come in. Don't just stand there, man,' Kevin Flynn said.

Bracken hesitated for a moment, his eyes boring into the younger man. Flynn was broad, like maybe he'd been a bricklayer at one time. His hair was well kept, his beard trimmed and no doubt well oiled, like an old bike. He was scattering things about his desk, obviously looking for something.

'You do know we're not on your payroll, right?' Bracken said.

That stopped the man in his tracks. His eyes were shiny, like he'd been crying, or maybe had something to bolster his confidence this morning.

'What are you wittering on about?' He stood up to his full height, which made him a couple of inches shorter than Bracken.

The big detective took a few steps into the room, followed by Sullivan.

'First of all, I don't *witter*, as you put it. I said, we're not on your payroll, so don't talk to us like we are. Sit down in your chair. We have some questions.'

Flynn looked at him like he wasn't hearing things correctly. Like maybe he had an ear infection and the words coming out of the big man's mouth weren't what was connecting in his ear.

'Sit down,' Bracken said again, this time with more force. Flynn complied.

The room was large but not overly so. There were two other chairs in front of the manager's desk, the last resting place of some unwary staff member who was about to be taken to the guillotine.

Bracken and Sullivan sat down opposite the man.

'I heard that you want to rearrange part of my anatomy?' Bracken said, staring at the man.

'I'm just hacked off. Nothing personal.'

'Let's not get off on the wrong foot here. I want to get straight to the point: a woman has been found dead in one of your offices. I want to know how that came about.'

Flynn sat back in his chair, wiping his hands down his face and over his beard. 'I really don't know. Honestly. We had a hen party in on Saturday night. A young woman with her friends. I had a few extra security on because you know how those things kick off. One minute they're having Sex on the Beach, the next they're having sex in the toilets. Or dancing on tables. Boxing with other people. You know how it goes. But overall, this lot were well behaved. Maybe because they come from money, I don't know.'

'How do you know they came from money?' Sullivan asked.

'I was talking to one of them. I mean, it's my job to be nice to people.'

'Including police officers?' Bracken said.

'Look, I'm sorry, okay? I could lose my job over this.'

'You were saying about mingling.'

'Yes. I was down there. I spoke to the bride-to-be, the chief bridesmaid. They were a nice lot. They had an open bar for their group, and the bride said she would put it on her credit card at the end of the night.

Well, come the end of the night, she'd skipped off. I'm left with a five-hundred-pound bill.'

'Did she seem upset? Meghan,' Sullivan said.

'No. She seemed happy and drunk and looking forward to getting married in a couple of weeks. They were going down to Barbados, she said. She didn't seem upset in the slightest.'

'No arguments between her and any of her friends?' Bracken said.

'Not that I saw. I was in the bar most of the night. It's a great place here, and we have blokes who can diffuse trouble, or handle it just as easily. But they're bouncers with brains, not like some of them who should be down a quarry breaking stones with a hammer.'

'Did any of her friends know she was missing?'

'They asked where she was, but one of them said she had gone off with a bloke. Some big bastard. Dressed smart but casual. That's all they remembered. They thought she was away to have a last fling.'

'You have cameras that cover down to the offices?' Bracken asked.

Flynn sat quietly for a moment. 'Just to the entrance to the club. And the back door that leads out into Rose Street Lane. It's heaving down there at the weekend. Most people use that entrance, but some come from the bar to go downstairs. It's a cattle market at times; that's why we have security.'

Bracken nodded. 'With such a lot of people, it could have been easy for somebody to slip past and go down to the next level where the offices are.'

He could tell Flynn was going to protest, but obviously it could happen because it had.

'I'm not making excuses, but we have a lot of people coming in and out. It's like Waverley Station at times. People laughing loudly, shrieking, clowning around. You name it, we see it. But we put up with it because a drunk parts with his or her money so much more easily, and we're in the business of making money, not running a nursery, looking after them...'

Bracken sensed the young man was losing it, so he put up a hand. 'I understand. But we still have the fact that somebody is dead downstairs, somebody who was a guest here and who shouldn't have been down there. She was seen with a stranger leaving her party, so we need to look at CCTV.'

'I know. Sorry. My assistant already has it ready to view in the security room. If you'll follow me.'

They got up and Flynn led them to a room further along the hallway. He barged in, skelping the door off the wall. A man in a suit sat at a console and wasn't fazed by the intrusion.

'Marco. These men are detectives. Show them

what they want to see.' Flynn looked at the officers. 'If you need to talk to me again, I'll be the one setting fire to his contract.'

He left, closing the door with less force than he had used to open it.

'Where do you want to start?' Marco asked.

'Around eleven p.m. Saturday night,' said Bracken. 'In the nightclub. I'll tell you when we see something.'

Marco nodded and started playing with the system. The footage on the screen was looking from the bar onto the dancefloor. They were looking for Meghan in her white dress and it took a few moments to pick her out.

'There!' Sullivan shouted.

Bracken looked at him, silently telling him that the room wasn't big, he wasn't deaf and somebody of a more nervous disposition might have had serious cardiac issues if they had been standing next to him.

'God help us all if we're playing bingo with you,' he said. Then, to the suit: 'There, son. That lassie in the white dress, surrounded by a bunch of her friends. Let it roll from there.'

The time stamp was three minutes past midnight, in the same ball park as the time Pam Green had given.

Men were approaching the women, some of them staying longer than others. They seemed to be having fun and the drink was flowing. The club was packed and it was difficult to keep up with Meghan as she got up to dance. Lights were flashing and the area where the tables were was in almost total darkness.

Then, as Meghan was standing at a table wrapped round a pillar, a tall man in a black suit approached. He was blond with a big build and he kept his face towards the floor as he made his way through the crowd. It would have been difficult to pick out his face in any case, and the flashing lights would have brought on a seizure if somebody was that way afflicted.

He whispered something to Meghan, and she followed him out of the club. Outside the entrance to the club was a short hallway with a set of doors, Bracken knew.

'Are there cameras that show the entrance to the offices down below the club?' he asked.

'No, they point from the entrance to the club to outside. Then there are the external ones, but otherwise the cameras are pointing to the entrance doors from Rose Street Lane.'

They watched as Meghan and the big man came out of the club and turned right towards the office doors.

'I wonder how he got through those office doors,' Sullivan said. 'I'm guessing they're locked after hours?'

'They are. I can't explain how they would have got in through there.'

'Keep rolling it forward,' Bracken said.

Marco did as instructed and figures were coming and going. They could see the bouncers at the back door controlling who came in. Then something happened. The two men ran out into the little court-yard of the club.

'What's happening there?' Bracken asked.

'It was some hooligans throwing bottles about and two landed in the courtyard,' Marco said.

'There we go. Look, our man is making his move,' Sullivan said.

The blond man walked with purpose, keeping his head low, and he left through the back door, following behind a few couples.

'Hiding in plain sight,' Bracken said, standing up straight. He patted Marco on the shoulder. 'Can we get a copy of that without a warrant?'

'Of course. If you give me an email address, I can send you a digital copy.'

Bracken handed him a business card that had his email on it.

They left the office and walked back down the stairs. Flynn was nowhere to be seen.

NINE

'Jimmy, you go ahead and I'll meet you downstairs,' Bracken said, taking his phone out. He waited until Sullivan had gone down the stairs before dialling a number.

'*Ed Bracken's office. Ed Bracken speaking. How may I help you?*'

'Are you going to answer the phone like that every time I call you?'

'*Maybe. Until I get fed up of doing it. Why?*'

'Because it's annoying. But Dad, listen, I need you to be serious now.'

'*Sorry, son. Carry on.*'

'Peter Fisher's daughter, Meghan; did she live at home, do you know?'

'*Christ, nothing's happened to her, has it?*'

'Dad, I just need to know. I can't say any more than that, I'm sorry.'

'*That's alright, son. Yes, she still lives there.*'

'Do you have Peter's details? Like a phone number. And do you know where he lives?'

'*I know he lives up at the Grange. I haven't been to his house in years. I have his mobile number, though.*'

Bracken listened to his father trying to find the number on his mobile, the one he was talking into at that moment, and inevitably he disconnected the call. Bracken hung up and waited for his dad to call back.

'*Bloody phones. How are you expected to look for something and talk at the same time? Anyway, here it is.*' Ed rattled off the number.

'Thanks. I'll be able to sit with you later and talk, but right now I have to talk to Peter.'

They said their goodbyes and Bracken hung up. Then he called the number.

'Mr Peter Fisher?'

'*Yes, speaking.*'

'I'm DCI Sean Bracken. I would like to come and talk to you, sir. Where can we meet?'

'*I'm at work just now. Is it important?*'

'It is.' *I'm about to change your life forever.*

Fisher told him where to come to. Bracken went in search of Sullivan.

TEN

'Peter Fisher works for the Scottish First Bank out at Gogarbank,' Bracken said to Kara when he was back downstairs.

All this exercise first thing in the morning was going to kill him. His plan to hit the gym in the New Year had hit the buffers early on, and all thought of getting up early to go speed-walking round the snow-covered streets in Corstorphine sounded about as appealing as...what? He couldn't think of anything. The exercise thing just couldn't get him out of bed in the morning. Get up and creep about in the dark or have another hour in bed? No contest.

'You'll never reach my age if you don't look after yourself,' his father had told him.

'That means I've got another twenty years of

having fun instead of eating rabbit food and wearing my knees out prematurely.'

'I hope you're still thinking that when some young doctor is slapping the paddles on your chest.' Ed had given up at that point.

Now Bracken was wondering why he was out of breath and that was from walking *downstairs*.

'Take Jimmy and Elsie. Go talk to Mr Fisher and find out if his daughter really did want out of her proposed marriage,' Kara said.

'We can take my car and you can leave your pool for DSup Page,' Bracken said to Jimmy, who handed over his keys.

'Right, which of you two is going to have the pleasure of driving me about?' Bracken said, nodding a goodbye to Chaz, who smiled at him.

'I can drive, sir,' Elsie said.

'Glad to hear it. I'll sit in the back and openly mock DI Sullivan for his lack of driving skills as I compare yours to his.'

'I'm a good driver,' Sullivan said.

'Says his mum. Come on, let's get out to Gogarbank. You know where that is, Elsie?'

'I do, sir.'

'Then let's do it. The sooner my car gets rolling, the sooner we can get some heat out of her.'

They headed out west, Elsie showing good driving skills.

'She's a good driver, Jimmy. I haven't reached for the invisible sick bag once so far.'

'That's bad form, boss, slagging off a senior officer in front of a detective of lower rank.'

'I'm just giving DC McDade a heads-up in case she ever finds herself in the passenger seat when you're driving.'

Sullivan put two fingers on the bridge of his nose.

'You okay there?' Bracken asked. 'I mean, if those are tears, you have to know I was just kidding.'

'Just thinking about that lassie.'

'Let's hear your thoughts.'

'Well, she's got everything going for her: rich daddy, nice area to live in according to her driving licence, and about to get married. If she was seeing somebody else, why not just call off the wedding? Why take her own life?'

'I was thinking the same. We need to find out if there is somebody else. Maybe her father will tell us.'

The snow had stopped and the main road was just wet after the salting it had been given. The bank was near the airport, on the west side of Edinburgh.

Elsie found a parking space near the door and they piled out. Men were out with little spreaders, walking back and forward, scattering salt.

Inside, it was obvious they threw caution to the wind when it came to their electric bill. The heat felt good, and it reminded Bracken of taking Sarah to the botanical gardens when she was little and going into the hothouse where they grew the tropical plants.

'DCI Sean Bracken,' he said, showing his warrant card. 'Peter Fisher is expecting us.'

They were shown up to an office that had a view over towards Edinburgh Airport. Peter Fisher was in his late sixties, if he was the same age as Ed Bracken, but he looked twenty years younger. Bracken didn't think Fisher would be out of breath going down the stairs.

There were diplomas on the wall and photographs sitting on a wall unit behind his desk. In one picture he had an arm around a younger woman. His wife, Bracken presumed.

'What can I do for you, DCI Bracken?' Fisher said.

It was obvious to Bracken that this man had no problems getting out of bed in the morning and going for a speed-walk through his neighbourhood.

'Wait a minute; you're Ed's son.'

'I am indeed. He told me about the party you gave on Saturday.'

'Yes, it was a special event. My daughter, Meghan, is getting married.'

Bracken looked at the photos on the wall unit and saw Meghan looking back at him. There was no doubt.

'I'm sorry to tell you this, Mr Fisher, but we found the body of a young woman this morning and we believe it to be that of your daughter, Meghan.'

Fisher sat back in his chair with a thump as if Bracken had punched him in the face.

'Meghan?' he said after a few moments, his voice barely a whisper. 'Meghan? No, that can't be right. She was at her hen party on Saturday night.'

'I'm sorry to say it is. I see her photo on your unit and we've just been with her.'

Fisher spun in his chair and looked at the photo before turning back to look at the detectives. 'My Meghan? Dead? How?' His eyes narrowed. 'How did she die?'

'It still has to be determined by the pathologist, but initial impressions are that she died of alcohol poisoning. And she left a note, apologising.'

'Alcohol poisoning? Note? You're not making sense.'

Bracken could see the colour had left the older man's face.

'It appears to be a suicide note. She said she was sorry but she couldn't go through with the wedding as she'd met somebody else, and it would seem it was all too much for her.'

'That's bollocks!' Fisher said, and Bracken recog-nised the signs: first the colour drains from the face, like the sea sweeping back from the shoreline just before the tsunami comes rushing in. 'Meghan was looking forward to getting married to Rodney. She was happy. They were in love. I can't believe she wrote a note like that.'

'We're trying to establish exactly what went on down there,' Sullivan said.

'Down where?'

'She was found dead in the offices of Checkers nightclub in George Street.'

'I know she was going there with her friends. How did she end up down in the offices?'

'We were hoping you could give us some insight into her state of mind,' Bracken said.

Fisher lifted a pencil in his right hand and started tapping the palm of his left hand.

'Did your daughter drink a lot?' Bracken said.

Fisher stopped tapping, and in that moment Bracken knew that the man was an alcoholic. The tapping of the pencil was a distraction. Maybe in the past he had run to a bottle and he was feeling the urge to do so now, but he was one pencil away from getting a glass out.

'Yes. She was a big drinker at one time. Now she just drank socially.'

'She would know that taking too much could affect her health,' Elsie said.

'She knew everything there was to know about binge drinking.'

'We think she had a lot to drink in the nightclub, then downed a bottle of vodka in the office,' Bracken said. 'But we're still looking into her death.'

'I can't believe it. Why would she do such a stupid thing? I told her not to be bloody stupid before she went out on Saturday. And why would she say she met somebody else?'

'Did she live at home?' Sullivan asked.

Fisher looked at him for a second as if his mind had hopped a train and it was pulling out of the station before he could put the brakes on.

'What? Oh. Yes. She and Rodney were going to buy a place after the wedding.'

'Where is Rodney now?'

'They were due back home later this morning. They had the stag do in Dublin.'

'I know this is hard, but we're going to have to talk to the women she was out with on Saturday, if you know their names,' Bracken said.

'Their contacts should be in her phone.'

'Her phone's missing. We're trying to get the phone company to track it. It might be switched off.'

Fisher looked around for a moment like he was

searching for a pen, then realised he had the pencil in his hand. He wrote something down, pulled the sheet off and slid it across the desk.

'That's Elaine's number. Elaine Norris. Meghan's best friend and maid of honour. I had it in case of emergency. The others were just a bunch of friends. Their numbers are on her phone.'

'Thank you. We're trying to trace her phone now.' Bracken pocketed the paper. 'Where did Meghan work?'

Fisher looked at him for a moment before answering. 'She was between jobs just now. She worked here for a while, but she was more of a free spirit. She wanted to start her own business but wasn't sure what she wanted to do.'

'We'd like you to come down to the city mortuary for an identification. I can have somebody drive you there if you like.'

Fisher shook his head. 'No. I have to go home and tell my wife.'

'If you could give us your details before you go, then we can contact you to see when it's convenient for you. Plus we'll have to speak with your wife later.'

'I don't want my wife interrogated, Inspector.'

'It's just a formality when there's a sudden death, I can assure you.'

'Very well. She's going to be devastated. They were very tight.'

The detectives stood up, but Fisher remained seated.

'We'll be in touch,' Bracken said, and as he was shutting the door behind him, he saw Fisher taking his mobile phone out.

'Poor sod,' Sullivan said.

'Aye, that can't be easy, getting news like that.' Bracken thought of his own daughter and it sent a shiver down his spine. If Mark Turner touched Sarah, Bracken would send more than a shiver down the boy's spine. He'd snap it.

ELEVEN

Elaine Norris told Bracken that she could meet him at lunchtime. He drove Sullivan and Elsie back to the station.

'How did Fisher take it?' Kara asked.

'He was in denial, of course. But he seemed to think his daughter had turned a corner. She had cut back on the drink and wasn't messing about with another man.'

'Not that his daughter would go around wearing a t-shirt proclaiming it if she was.'

'Well, if she was cheating, she was hiding it very well.' Bracken sipped the cup of coffee he was holding.

'How's the new girl holding up?'

'So far she's been fine. If this case turns out to be anything but a suicide, then we'll see if she cracks under pressure.'

'I'm hoping she can hold her own. She was good in CID in Inverness.'

Bracken looked at his watch. 'As you know, I'm on the transition team for Ailsa Connolly's release. I'd like to go and talk to her husband. Then talk to her.'

'That's fine. Are you expected up there?'

'No, but I can go in anytime. They said the more unexpected, the better.'

'I'll keep you posted when we hear anything. The postmortem was getting started right away. Izzie and Sullivan just left.'

Bracken grabbed his jacket and made his way downstairs to the small car park at the back of the building at Haymarket. The West End station was in need of an overhaul, and maybe one day they would get round to it, but Bracken couldn't see it happening, not with all the police stations that were being closed down.

It had started snowing again. The sky was the colour of a grumpy old man.

He tuned the car radio in to a local station, but it was only background noise as he thought about Ailsa Connolly.

She was a psychologist, and a killer. He had thought he was about to become her seventh victim, but recent events had cast doubt on that. The fact that she was a serial killer was never in doubt, though.

She had been looking at spending the rest of her life in the new secure wing of the Royal Edinburgh after it was thought she had murdered some kids. That turned out to be false. Another killer had confessed to those murders, so now Ailsa was eligible for release after it had been argued that she had killed while not of sound mind.

It hadn't hindered her that she and the Scottish justice minister went way back. But an American author and psychologist, Edwin Hawk, had given her an unbiased evaluation and deemed her fit for release.

Now they were in the transition period. They weren't just going to open the door and bid her farewell. Bracken, who had caught her, was on the team to make sure he still held the opinion that she should be released. They figured that if she was going to pull the wool over anybody's eyes, it would be the people who knew her.

Ailsa had got married the week before Christmas, to a former colleague. Now, Robert Marshall worked as a psychologist at the Royal Edinburgh and lived just round the corner from the hospital.

Bracken drove in silence for the last leg of the drive and pulled up outside the house in Morningside. Marshall's Beetle sat in the driveway in front of the garage.

'Come in, Sean!' the man shouted from within the house. The front door was ajar.

'Bit iffy that, isn't it?' Bracken said, stepping into the warmth and closing the door behind him.

'What's that?' Marshall said, coming into the hallway from the kitchen.

'Leaving your bloody door open, that's what!' Bracken stamped his feet on the mat and took his overcoat off, then hung it on a hook.

'I saw you coming. The kettle has been on since you said you were coming over.' Marshall was leaning heavily on his walking stick.

'Fair enough.'

'The mugs are ready, if you wouldn't mind. There's a packet of rich teas in the cupboard.'

'Good God, Robert. How desperate do you think I am?'

'For a biscuit or...'

'Don't start analysing me,' Bracken said, walking to the kitchen. He returned to the living room with the two mugs and handed one to Marshall.

'I'm kidding. Chaz Cullen is a very nice lady. You could do a lot worse.'

Bracken sat down. 'How dare you. We're just friends.'

Marshall laughed and took a sip of the hot coffee. 'I'm hardly one to dish out marriage advice, but so far

Ailsa and I are happy. I still have lunch with her every day. Even managed to sneak in a quick conjugal visit one day.'

'I'm not supposed to hear this stuff.'

'Relax. I'm kidding. You know I can't move fast.'

'I'm on the team who are monitoring the situation, remember? In fact, that's why I came round,' Bracken said.

'I thought it was because you wanted me to teach you how to play chess.'

'Moving wee bits of wood around a board painted with squares. That's a waste of TV time, Robert.'

Marshall shook his head. 'It will train your brain, Sean. Not that it needs trained, but it will help you think of a problem in a different way.'

'Still. Little wooden pieces.' Bracken shrugged like he was imagining the pieces on a bonfire, where they belonged.

'They can be made of other things too, you know. Not just wood.'

'Maybe one day.'

'You don't mean that.'

'I do,' Bracken said. 'I haven't closed the door on the possibility.'

They sat in silence for a moment.

'How is Chaz after our ordeal?' Marshall asked.

Chaz and some others, including Bob Long and Marshall, had been taken hostage by a killer.

'She's still having a rough time of it, if I'm honest.'

'All the more reason for you to keep an eye on her. She's terrific. If I was your age and not quite as decrepit —'

'Or married.'

'Or married, I would love to step out with the lovely Miss Cullen.'

'Are you one of those people who think a bloke can't be friends with a woman without thinking he's signing up for the gold package?' Bracken said.

'Now, you know me better than that, Sean. I believe that anybody can be friends with anybody. If a man can be friends with a woman and not feel sexual attraction, then that's perfectly acceptable.'

'You're smiling,' Bracken said.

'What's wrong with that?' Marshall drank more of his coffee.

'It means the wheels are turning in your head. It means you want to give me some dating advice but indirectly.'

'You're very astute.'

'I'm very experienced. I sit across the table from a lot of people who try to convince me that they're inno-cent. They play head games, trying psychology.

They're not as good as you, Robert, but you get the idea.'

Marshall gave a short laugh. 'I'm sorry. Here's me trying to be a matchmaker when all you want to be is a friend to her. That's not a bad idea, though. She needs you right now, whether as a friend or more.'

'Are you coping with it? After all, they did come into your house here and take you away.'

'I'm fine. I teach people how to have a mental toolbox that they can open up and use to cope with different things. Then compartmentalise things. Put them into a mental filing cabinet, if you will. I have my little box under mental lock and key, Sean, don't worry.'

'You're a remarkable man, if I may say so.'

'Of course you may. I won't take it as you patronising me. But instead of talking about Miss Cullen, how about we get to the point?'

Bracken looked puzzled. 'What point is that?'

'Oh, come on now, Sean. You came here like you sometimes do, but today is different: you want to ask me if things are still the same with Ailsa. If she's still doing well and heading in the right direction. The answer is yes. Her mental health is good and she's not the same woman she was six years ago. Her mind merely slipped a couple of gears, but now the engine is running just fine.'

'You know I like coming round here, Robert, but I just wanted to bring it into the conversation before I go round and see her.'

'I know you did, and that's fine. I have some spare time on my hands until I hold a meeting this evening. AA meeting. I'm working on a book just now.'

'Non-fiction?'

'It is. Ailsa wants me to write her story one day, but for now I'm working on another psychology book. It's about manipulation and how you can get somebody to think the same way you do.'

'That's something you must have seen a lot of through the years,' Bracken said.

'I have. And it's not about Ailsa in any way. It's based on some of the stories I've heard during my career. I'll put in fake names, of course. Some people are very clever, you know. Especially children. No matter what age, some of them can twist their parents around their little fingers, let me tell you. They're the worst.'

'I never let my Sarah get away with anything,' Bracken said, in case this was a slight against his parenting skills.

'Not your daughter, Sean. I'm talking about the bad ones. The little angels who can do no wrong but who go on to murder people. Little bastards.' Marshall chuckled. 'Some people would be shocked to hear me say that, given that I'm a psychologist who gets paid to help people, but some just can't be helped, and I've dealt with the dregs of society.'

'Does it ever make you want to abstain from drinking? Talking at an alcoholics' meeting?'

'Hell, no. It makes me glad I'm a drinker. I like my wee dram, Sean. It keeps me sane at times. What about you? Ever regret drinking?'

'Not in the slightest. It's a Scottish sport, isn't it? We would win gold every time if it were an Olympic sport.'

'This is true.'

Bracken hadn't seen Marshall since the trouble with his father being abducted and his home being set on fire, so he updated him.

'You were both very lucky,' Marshall said.

'I had two good officers with me: Jimmy Sullivan and my old DI from Fife, Cameron Robb. Two men I would have in my corner every time.'

'And now I know at first hand how good it is to have somebody you trust fighting in your corner.' Marshall looked at Bracken. 'We could all have been killed that day. You put your life on the line to save us.'

'It's my job.'

'It was more than that. You put your life on the line without thinking twice about it.'

'I did what had to be done.'

Marshall smiled. 'Let me ask you: did you do it because it was merely your job, or did you feel that subconscious need to save a loved one?'

'None of my family members were there.'

'That's not what I said. I used the term *loved one*. There's a difference. Subtle sometimes, but there. The primeval urge to save your mate. Who was there when we were abducted? Chaz.'

Bracken finished his coffee, then stood up. 'Talking of loved ones, I'm going round to see yours.'

Marshall laughed. 'On the way over, think about what I said.'

'Keep your bloody front door locked, Robert. See you soon.'

It was bitterly cold outside with a chill wind whipping along the quiet street in Morningside, but Bracken didn't feel it. There were so many other things going through his mind.

Marshall was just talking pish, wasn't he? Trying to bamboozle him with psychological mumbo jumbo.

He got in his car for the two-minute drive to the Royal Edinburgh psychiatric hospital.

TWELVE

Bracken sat in his car, turning the fan speed down but keeping the heating on. He was daft but not that daft. He and his ex-wife were at opposite ends of the spectrum when it came to heat in the house. Catherine always had a window open and a fan blowing, even in winter. She was a *freeze the nuts off a polar bear* type, whereas he was very much in favour of inviting the polar bear in for a cup of hot chocolate and a seat by the log fire. At that moment, sitting in his roasting car, she would have been in her underwear if it wouldn't have got her arrested. Not by him, but by some passing polis with an attitude and a pair of handcuffs.

He pressed the telephone button on the steering wheel and listened to the tinny sound of Catherine's phone ringing somewhere in outer space. He assumed that was where she was, as the sound of her phone could compete with waterboarding when it came to torture. He'd get better reception from a machine sending back photos from Mars.

Finally, she answered, sounding like she was talking through her space suit.

'Hello? Sean? Is everything okay?'

'Yes, nothing to worry about. I was wondering if you were free for lunch?'

'What's the occasion?'

'Nothing. I just thought it would be nice.'

'Ah, right. I see.' Said in the tone you might use when somebody had pissed the bed and was blaming it on a leaky hot water bottle.

'I'm paying. You can choose where we go.'

Silence for a moment. Maybe she was doing a Google search for the most expensive restaurant she could reach from her bank branch, given that she had an hour and there was travelling time included.

'Loon Fung Cantonese?' she eventually said, giving up any hope of getting down to The Kitchin and back in an hour. 'One o'clock?'

Bracken looked at the dashboard clock. 'Any chance of one thirty? I have to interview somebody first.'

'Being the manager, I can swing that.'

'Good. I'll see you inside. Unless, you know, you enjoy the cold.'

'Shut up, Sean.'

He chuckled as he hung up. Then turned off the engine and stepped out into Catherine's ideal weather. She had said she could quite easily live in a cold country, or the northeast of America, whereas he would be quite happy sitting on a beach in Key West.

Opposites attract.

He trudged through the snow of the car park and into the entrance of the new wing of the Royal Edinburgh. The wing held Category A prisoners, including Ailsa Connolly, who was the only female being held and had a small suite to herself.

He shook off the snow and stamped his boots on a rubber mat.

A woman behind the Plexiglas window – which may or may not have been bulletproof, Bracken thought – tutted at him as the automatic sliding door engaged in a battle of wits with him. He stepped forward in victory and approached the window.

'My name is DCI Sean Bracken –' he started to say before the woman interrupted him with an exaggerated tut.

'I know who you are. I may be old, but they're not reserving a room for me upstairs just yet.'

'Can you buzz me through then?'

'Manners.'

Bracken smiled and gritted his teeth. *Just imagine*

she's your granny, he told himself, holding back a response that may have been appropriate but would have been scolding at the same time.

'Please,' he said in a low voice.

'Now say it like you mean it.'

Bracken raised his eyebrows at her and once again she tutted. Then she pushed whatever it was that had to be pushed in order to open the sliding door next to the window.

He paused, straddling the threshold. 'You know, when the zombie apocalypse strikes, you'll be thankful for people like me.'

'I know I will; they'll have plenty to chew on when they get you. They'll ignore some grizzled old bag like me. Now, if you don't mind, you're causing a draught.'

Bracken turned away from her and walked in, thinking that he had only lost the battle, not the war. This wasn't his first dealing with the woman, and it wouldn't be the last. But he had to remember she was somebody's grandmother. Poor bastard.

Upstairs, it was obvious the old woman had called the clinical director, no doubt hoping she was ratting Bracken out over something.

'Ah, DCI Bracken. Good to see you again,' Fritz Meyer said, smiling at him and holding out a hand to shake.

'Likewise, Doctor,' Bracken said.

'Ailsa's been in good spirits. Not surprising considering we're in the transition period between her being incarcerated and walking among the living again. Come, let's walk along to her suite.'

'Who will take her place in there?' Bracken asked as Meyer scanned his pass through electronically locked doors. Bracken wondered how far he would get right now if he snatched the card and started swiping at each door. Would somebody sitting in front of a monitor hit a big red button to stop him? He was too tired to try it anywhere but in his mind.

'It depends on who we have coming here. If it's another female then it will stay the same, but if it's a male then it will be changed. We have no timeline yet, but as you know we expect Ailsa to be released within the next month.'

Another door, another buzz, another click as it locked behind them. Then they were in the hallway that led to Ailsa's suite.

Meyer unlocked the door and was met by an orderly. The man Bracken had had a previous encounter with wasn't present.

One more door and they were into the suite itself. The room had been made to look like a living room, with a bedroom and bathroom off it. Both rooms had doors that swung inwards to the living room with easy-access hinges that could be popped in a second.

Ailsa was sitting at a small desk, reading a book.

'Hello, Sean,' she said, beaming a smile at him. 'I'm catching up with some Friedrich Nietzsche. I promise I'm not looking into the abyss.'

'Interesting how his first name is spelled *Fried Rich*. Maybe somebody in the family had an aspiration for what they wanted to do to wealthy people but named the boy that instead,' Bracken said.

'He was named after Friedrich Wilhelm the Fourth of Prussia,' Meyer interjected as if Bracken had slighted him. 'The Nietzsche family weren't poor.'

'I know. I was attempting banter, which crashed and burned apparently,' Bracken said. Then, to Ailsa: 'You mind if I take my coat off? I don't want to drip all over your expensive Persian rug.' He turned to Meyer, who merely nodded.

'Banter *and* sarcasm,' Meyer said. 'One wonders what the trifecta would be.'

Bracken couldn't think of a third thing and wondered what Meyer would make of it if he set fire to the curtains.

'Do you think we could rustle up some coffee for DCI Bracken?' Ailsa asked.

'I will personally organise it,' Meyer said, smiling. He left the suite while Bracken hung his coat on a stand that was rounded at the top. While it wouldn't exactly stab somebody, it could certainly be used to give somebody like him a sore pair of testicles. That was why it was screwed to the floor.

'Sit down, Sean. Tell me what's happening in your life.'

While technically it wasn't supposed to work this way, Bracken nevertheless took the weight off his feet and let her take control of the conversation. He sat on a leather chair opposite her.

'Same old, I'm afraid,' Bracken said. 'How about you?'

'I'm delighted to say that we found a minister of the Church who is willing to take me under his wing for fifteen months after I'm released and graduate.'

'That's good news. But aren't you worried that your new congregation will be scared to come to one of your sermons?' Bracken said.

'What, in case I pull out a chainsaw and have at it? No, there are wee churches in the middle of nowhere that haven't seen the benefit of electricity yet and don't know television has been invented, and they'll welcome me with open arms.'

Bracken looked like he was searching his memory bank for where such a place could be but was coming up nil.

'I'm kidding, Sean. I meant there are rural communities who will be only too happy to have me as their minister.'

'I bet you won't get mugged.'

'You mean because I'll be a minster, or...'

'No, I mean you'll put the fear of God into them in more ways than one.'

She laughed. 'I'll be using my middle name and I'll be Mrs Marshall.'

'Good idea.'

'I know you have to pop in for a wee chat every so often and get an update on my behaviour, but I'd like to think you were here because you enjoy my company.'

'All work and no play? How would that make you feel?' he asked her.

'I would be disappointed, but I know you, Sean. I knew you back then, when you were first sent to me.'

Bracken took in a deep breath and let it out through his nose.

'Billy Turner,' she said, her voice low. 'The bank robber you shot dead. That's why you and your team were sent to me. To make sure you were coping with it.'

'I was coping with it just fine,' he replied, his voice rising slightly.

'It wasn't a slight on your manhood. People react differently when taking a human life in the course of their work. You seemed to be okay. And by that, I mean you didn't rejoice in the fact, but you knew you'd done what had to be done at the time.'

He had to admit, Ailsa was good. Just by watching

his body language she had jumped on the fact that Billy Turner was on his mind, or rather, his son was.

'It's his son, Mark, who's bothering me now.'

She sat up slightly straighter. It was such a subtle movement, like something a cat would do, but his trained eye noticed it. It was something feral that an experienced copper learned to spot over time. Sometimes it was a precursor to an attempt to end a copper's life. Just like in a jungle, sometimes you only had a split second to react.

But in this jungle setting, Ailsa was sitting ten feet away from him. It was a distance that had been calculated when placing the furniture. Somebody figured that it would take a few seconds for her to get up from the chair and launch herself at a visitor. That was why the chair she was sitting on was sagging at the back and the one he was sitting on was stiff with more padding. Time to get up and counteract any attack. Those were the rules: she had to sit in that chair when she had a visitor, or else there would be no visitors.

'Tell me about his son,' she said, and in Bracken's mind it was like a growl from a big cat.

'He was seeing my daughter. As a friend, but she wanted more than that. She liked him, he was well presented, and she wanted me to meet him. So I did, before New Year.'

'And let me guess: Baby Bear brought along a play-mate and Daddy Bear showed his teeth.'

'Och, you know me, Ailsa.'

'I do. That's why I said it.'

'Aye, I suppose I did, but he only managed to make it to the toilets before I pissed off my daughter. They left. But he looked at me in a way I recognised: he knew me. He didn't think I knew him, but I had a friend check him out and that's what we discovered.'

'Is she still seeing him?'

Bracken smiled, but there was no warmth there. It was a smile that promised an adversary a kicking. He furrowed his brow and clamped his teeth together. 'Oh, no.'

'Sean, relax. Your blood pressure just went through the roof. I can tell just by looking at you. And I'm willing to bet the adrenaline just kicked in as well.'

He took a few breaths; in through the nose, out through the mouth. 'It's no coincidence that he was seeing her as a friend and then dumped her after that meeting.'

'You and I both know it wasn't a coincidence.'

'I know. She said he was a student, but he isn't registered anywhere.'

'Keep an eye on her, Sean. Tell her to be careful.'

'Way ahead of you there.'

'Meyer's coming back with the coffee. I can hear the door opening.'

'Quick question: you honestly believe you can cope with the outside world now?'

'I do. I have Robert by my side. We're going to start our new life together, and you played a part in that by catching that killer. I won't dignify him by using his name.'

'He's having a hard time in Carstairs,' Bracken said.

'I know. It's not my problem.'

Fritz Meyer came in with three polystyrene cups of lukewarm coffee. Nothing that could be used as a weapon.

'Here we go. Three cups of coffee.'

'Café mocha with whipped cream?' Ailsa asked.

'They were all out of mocha. However, this is the Royal Edinburgh's finest instant. Extra milk.'

'You do spoil me, Fritz.'

'Don't tell everybody.'

He sat down ten feet away from Ailsa after dishing out the cups. 'How are things with you, Detective Bracken?' Meyer asked.

'You can call me Sean. I'm living the quiet life. How about you?'

'Ah, you know how it is: bank account is crying after Christmas, I've put on weight and the New Year's resolution to take up jogging has yet to take flight.'

'Ailsa is looking forward to getting out, even though it will be under licence to begin with,' Bracken said. 'I want to assure her that she will be given all the help she needs to transition into a new life.'

'That's what we're all here for. You, me, the committee. Stuart MacDonald.'

MacDonald, the justice minister.

'Not everybody is going to be happy that she's being released, and when the press get wind of it, she'll be haunted by them.'

'That's why no press release is going to be issued, I can assure you,' Meyer said. 'Ailsa and Robert can start their new life away from here, but they will still have support. You or a team member might have to travel to wherever they are to provide support of a law enforcement nature.'

'A special team will be put together and we'll be at their disposal,' Bracken assured him.

'Good. Now, Ailsa, you're going out on day release at the end of the week with DSup Kara Page. There will be no notice given, and you'll be driven to the church where you'll meet the minister. Nobody will know who you are, and you can have a relaxing day getting a feel for what it's like to be in charge of a church. "Public integration," I believe Stuart MacDonald called it. Are you ready for it?'

'I am. I feel the Church is my life now and I'm very much looking forward to it.' She smiled at Meyer.

'You have no qualms, Chief Inspector?' he said.

'None at all. Not when DSup Page is going to be behind the wheel for Ailsa's protection.'

'Good. Then we're all on board about what needs to happen. I won't be there, but you'll be in good hands, Ailsa.'

They drank their coffee and chatted about what was going on in the world.

After a while, Bracken looked at his watch. 'I have to be going. I have a meeting.' *Lunch meeting.*

Bracken and Meyer stood up while Ailsa remained seated. Another protocol.

Meyer's phone rang and he answered it, spoke briefly and hung up. 'I have to go. Problems elsewhere.' He shook Bracken's hand. 'Don't be a stranger.'

'Take care, Dr Meyer.'

The clinical director grabbed the cups and left the room.

'Did they catch whoever set fire to Kara Page's house?' Ailsa asked as Bracken sat back down. He checked his watch. Another five minutes wouldn't do any harm.

'No, we still don't have a lead yet.'

'I spoke to Edwin Hawk after he did his evaluation on me. He had an interesting theory. You know that two men tried to kill me, you and the others. Hawk believes there's a third person still out there whom you don't know about.'

Bracken sat silently for a few moments before speaking. 'That's what I think too. I don't think this is over.'

THIRTEEN

'Half an hour before they stop serving lunch,' Catherine Bracken said as Bracken entered the Loon Fung Cantonese restaurant in Canonmills.

'I don't think they'll kick us out at two on the dot. I know a food hygiene inspector at the council. I'll name-drop if I have to.'

'I didn't know that.'

'There's a lot you don't know about me.'

'Really. Most people name-drop celebrities, but my ex-husband knows somebody who will prove far more interesting to the owner of this restaurant.'

'This old dog still has a few surprises up his sleeve,' Bracken said with a hint of pride in his voice.

'Hardly old. You make me feel old when you talk like that and I'm a few years younger than you.'

The waiter showed them to a table, smiling at Catherine, the regular, with her new beau.

'Miss Catherine. How are you today?'

'Just peachy, Wan, thank you. And yourself?'

'Stocks going up, thank you,' he said with a big smile, scooting away to get the menus.

There were several other couples in the restaurant and Bracken admitted to himself that it felt good to be here with Catherine again, and then he got hit with a little jolt of anger. Thinking back to when his wife had cheated on him.

Then he did what Robert Marshall had talked about and compartmentalised it. Smiled at her, because after all, she was here at his invite.

The waiter came back and they ordered their food, lemon chicken for Bracken and chicken chow mein for Catherine, and a couple of soft drinks.

'This is a nice change, Sean. We haven't done this in years.' The waiter brought their drinks over and Catherine looked at Bracken. 'So what's on your mind?'

'Does there have to be a reason to invite you to lunch?'

'Yes.'

'Whoa, where did that attack come from?' he said in mock indignation.

Catherine smiled. 'Always the clown. But remember, the clock is ticking, said the prossie to the vicar.'

'Okay, you got me. Jeez, if you would just let me get a word in, I could talk to you.'

'Sean, I know my branch is just across the road in Brandon Terrace, two minutes' walk from here, but this conversation could go on forever.'

'I'm worried about Sarah,' he said. 'Did she tell you I saw her on Saturday night?'

'With your girlfriend, yes. What's her name again? Jizz or something?'

'Oh, come on, that was low, even for you. Chaz, and she's not my girlfriend. We just hang out, have a drink sometimes as colleagues. Nothing more.'

The waiter brought their food. It hadn't taken long and Bracken knew they served good food. They thanked Wan and he left them in peace.

'She seems nice, according to our daughter,' Catherine said.

'Which one? Jizz or Chaz?'

'Seriously. If she decides that she likes you, you should hang on to her.'

'I know I don't exactly have women beating a path to my door, but I do alright,' Bracken said. He picked at the food, not quite hungry.

'Save it for the judge, Chief Inspector.'

'It's true. I don't go home at night and lock myself in my room, playing *Mario Kart*.'

'How's Ed doing?'

'He's fine. A bit shaken up after the fire, but he has Max to keep him company.'

'Tell him I said hi, Sean. I don't see him much, but I still love him. And you'd bloody well better look after him.'

'I will. And I do. But we're getting a bit off topic here, Catherine. I'm worried.'

'What are you worried about? Sarah's an independent young woman. She can look after herself.'

'I know she can, but she was friends with some young bloke who isn't what he was pretending to be.'

'Just like that boy's dad when Sarah was in primary school. You thought he was a paedo, but it turned out he was just a photographer.'

'Listen, I still think that bastard's dodgy. I can't prove it, but you mark my words...' He ate a little bit of chicken.

'What's worrying you this time? That this young bloke is keeping her up past her curfew?'

'I just know members of his family, and despite his hoity-toity accent, he's as rough as they come.'

'Rougher than a badger's arsehole? Isn't that what you usually say?'

'I'm in the company of a lady,' Bracken said. 'She's sitting over there, behind you.'

'Still with the dynamite humour, I see.' She gave a wry smile and ate some of her own chicken. 'What is it that bothers you? You think this young guy was messing her about? If he was, then she should think herself lucky she had a narrow escape.'

'His name is Mark Turner.'

Catherine stopped for a second and looked him in the eye. 'Billy Turner's son?'

'The very same.'

'Are you sure?'

He gave her a look with raised eyebrows.

'Of course you're sure. Sean Bracken doesn't jump to conclusions. But don't you think it could just be a coincidence?'

'No. It's a cliché, I know, that coppers don't think anything is a coincidence, but this time I believe it.'

'Did you tell Sarah when you saw her?'

Bracken shook his head. 'I didn't want to scare her. I just told her to be on her guard.'

'Maybe it's nothing.' Catherine didn't sound convinced.

'Let's hope.' He ate a little more of the chicken. 'How's Stan doing these days?'

'Stan decided that the grass was greener. A barmaid from Juniper Green.'

'Sorry to hear that.' Bracken could easily have said that it was what she deserved, to be cheated on, but he couldn't do that. The bitterness and anger were left far behind now, with only the occasional foray into self-pity. Stan had been Catherine's long-term boyfriend, and he was genuinely sorry that the man had decided to look elsewhere for something he wasn't getting out of his relationship.

Then Bracken's phone rang. He took it out of his pocket and looked at the screen. 'Sorry, I have to take this.'

'It's okay.'

'Hello?'

'I'm looking for a tall, dark, handsome stranger, but you'll have to do,' Chaz said.

'I'm actually having a business lunch just now.'

'Oh, sorry. I just thought you would like to know that we got the tox reports back for Meghan Fisher. She had enough sleeping tablets in her system to kill an elephant.'

'Christ, really?'

'Yes, really. You might want to talk to forensics and see if there were any empty packets of sleeping tablets on her person or in her handbag.'

'How many would be a lethal dose?'

'The active ingredient was diphenhydramine. Dr Green said five hundred mills could kill some people,

depending on their body weight. Meghan weighed over eight stone, or around a hundred and twenty-five pounds for the sake of the weight-to-drug-intake ratio. There was around two thousand milligrams of diphen-hydramine in her system, plus she had a blood alcohol level of over three point one per cent. Well blootered; probably would have died of alcohol poisoning or close to it.'

'Does Dr Green have an exact cause of death yet?'

'Not yet. She's still working on the p.m. as we speak. Izzie and the new girl are here. DC McDade.'

'Thanks, Chaz.'

'Aye-aye, Captain. Bridge out.'

He hung up and put his phone away.

'Your friend Chaz,' Catherine said. It wasn't a question.

'How did you know?'

'You just said, "Thanks, Chaz."'

'I would trip myself up if I was getting interviewed by the polis,' he said.

'You would. They wouldn't have to beat you with a hose and throw you down some stairs. You would act like a dimwit and give them what they wanted to know. And that's before they even threatened to pull your teeth.'

'You know me so well.'

'Anyway, please don't scare Sarah. I'll have a talk

with her. But realise something: she's a copper's daughter. She's not stupid.'

'I know.'

They finished their lunch and chitchatted about other events, Bracken's mind on a man who may or may not be targeting him.

And what he was going to do about it.

FOURTEEN

Bracken called Elaine Norris and apologised for being late. She told him it was fine and to meet her any time before five.

She was a photographer and artist and worked from home in her mews house in Circus Lane. It was a five-minute drive from Canonmills and Bracken parked right at her front door. The façade was painted a muted shade of yellow and there was a plant pot either side of the front door. A garage door was painted the same colour.

The snow was thicker here, and Bracken wondered how many times a plough would come along here.

Elaine Norris opened the front door wearing an over-sized knitted cardigan. Her hair was short and straight, but it was the red eyes he noticed. He showed her his warrant card.

'Come in, please,' she said, stepping aside. A ginger cat stood looking at Bracken from along the lobby. He walked through to the back, where the living room was. It was surprisingly big. From the outside, the mews houses almost looked like doll houses.

'Peter Fisher called you, I take it?' Bracken said.

She nodded. 'He did. I can't believe it.'

'Can you tell me a little bit about the last time you saw Meghan on Saturday night?'

She offered him a seat on the couch and Ginger jumped on the back. He put a hand out for it to sniff before it got the idea to sharpen its claws on his head.

Elaine sat on a chair. There were photos of Edinburgh and New York in frames on the wall. No personal photos.

'We were bar-hopping, but behaving ourselves,' she said. 'We were having a laugh and getting slowly drunk.'

'Did anybody bother you in any of those places?'

Elaine shook her head. 'There were guys coming up to us and having a laugh, and they were fine.'

'What about the guy in Checkers nightclub?'

'He was talking to Meghan for a little while. We were all talking to people, as well as having a laugh in the group. I was ready to call it a night, to be honest. I'm not much of a drinker now. Bit of a lightweight.'

'Did you talk to this man?' Bracken asked. 'The one with the blond hair?'

She shook her head. 'He wasn't interested in talking to anybody else except Meghan. After a little while, I turned round and they were gone.'

'Did that surprise you?' Bracken asked.

'It did. But she seemed to like him.'

'Meghan didn't work, her father said. How did she spend her days?'

'She was trying to open an interior design place of her own. She was very creative and her mother would have helped her financially. Her dad works for the bank, but the family has money.'

Bracken was glad Ginger wasn't taking a Benny with his head and had plopped down onto the arm of the settee instead.

'Meghan left a suicide note, apologising to her fiancé about cheating on him. She had a boyfriend,' Bracken said.

Elaine's eyes widened. 'Boyfriend? Meghan? Not a chance in hell. I was her best friend. I would have known if she was cheating.'

'Sometimes even best friends don't admit they're cheating.'

'Rodney's a fantastic man. He's got a great personality, he's good-looking and he owns his own business. She would never cheat on him.'

'Why do you think she would leave a suicide note saying she *was* cheating?'

'I have no idea, honestly.'

'Do you think it could have been with this man who took her down to the offices below the club?' Bracken said, moving his eyes sideways when Ginger stood up and arched its back before sitting back down again to do some face washing with the lick of a paw.

'They were talking, and yes, it could be interpreted that she knew him. I didn't see much of his face, though. It was dark, plenty of flashing lights. Prince William could have been in there and nobody would have noticed. One minute she was there, and the next they were gone. I thought she had gone to the toilet at first, but she didn't come back. I was worried about her and texted her, but there was no reply. To be honest, I thought she knew the guy and had left with him. I was hoping they had just gone up to the bar for another drink.'

'What about the end of the night?'

'I was disappointed, but she's a grown woman. I didn't hear from her on Sunday and didn't call because I knew she was probably working off a hangover.'

'Understandable.' He paused for a moment, hoping his sentiment sounded real and not made-up polis pish. 'Do you have contact numbers for your other friends? We're having a problem tracing her phone.'

Elaine shook her head. 'They weren't mutual friends. I don't have many friends of my own. Meghan was my good friend. I didn't know the others. I can't remember their names now. I got introduced, but after the amount of drink I had, I've forgotten them. I barely spoke to them all night.'

Elaine started crying again. 'Christ, if I'd only known she was down below us in those offices.'

'There was no way for you to know.' He waited for a couple of minutes while she blew her nose into a hanky, thanking God he hadn't lent her one. 'Are you married?' he said her.

'No. Why?'

'Just so I could make a call if you wanted me to. Anybody else? Partner?'

'No. There's nobody.'

Bracken thanked her and stood up just as Ginger got to licking a part of its anatomy that only a feline can. He was glad the cat didn't want a kiss goodbye.

'If you remember anything else, please call me,' he said, handing Elaine a card. Then Ginger meowed a *big bastard* at him as he left.

FIFTEEN

Bracken sat in the dining room with his dad, not eating but not wanting to be a Norrie Nae Mates by sitting in the lounge on his own. He'd broken the news about Meghan to Ed earlier.

'Cheer up, son,' Ed said. 'You look like somebody stole your ball.' He was tucking into mince and tatties.

'Just something bothering me,' Bracken said. 'About a case. Well, it's not exactly an MIT case, but CID threw it our way after they found out the name of the victim.'

'Run it by me. Maybe I'll have some constructive criticism.'

'The same way you tell me I drink too much and should be married again at my age?'

'No, no. That's different. That's me being a parent. This is now Ed, the critical thinker.'

Natalie Hogan was sitting at another table with her eight-year-old son, Rory.

'You might as well get in on this, Natalie,' Bracken said. 'Being an ex-doctor.'

'Why not? It beats people asking me where they can find the baked beans.'

Ed pointed a fork at his son. 'Just because she's been struck off, doesn't mean to say she's no longer a doctor. I mean, which one of us do you think is going to give you mouth-to-mouth if you collapse right now?'

'Good point.' Bracken turned to Natalie. 'If you see him on his knees beside me when I'm lying on the carpet, slap him.'

'Never going to happen,' Ed said with conviction. 'I'll say a prayer, though. Maybe give a wee eulogy telling people how you used to show me respect and treated me well. Before...you know....you went off your heid.'

'Oh, shut up.'

Ed looked at Natalie. 'Proves my point, eh?'

'Can we just concentrate?'

'If you're finished your dinner, you can go and watch some TV in the lounge before homework,' Natalie told Rory, who smiled and left the table with no arguments.

'Right,' Bracken said when he had their attention. 'This young woman is on her hen night with her pals.

She has a good amount to drink, then she wanders off with this bloke, who we can't identify. He takes her down to the offices below the nightclub, maybe to have sex, but there's no evidence of that. She has a tremendous amount of alcohol and takes some sleeping tablets, enough to kill her, but in any case, she's had enough alcohol to kill her. She leaves a note to her future husband, apologising and explaining she's been seeing somebody else.' He looked at them. 'Over to you. Talk amongst yourselves.'

'When are they getting married?' Natalie asked.

'Valentine's Day,' Ed answered, then shoved some tatties into his mouth.

Bracken looked at her. 'My dad knows this woman's father. He was at a party on Saturday night celebrating the young couple's upcoming wedding. Lucky old bugger. He gets out more than I do.'

Natalie nodded. 'They're getting married in a few weeks and she's at her hen night, but she decides to kill herself and leave a note in a strange club? This doesn't ring true.'

'It doesn't make sense,' Bracken agreed. 'People tend to commit suicide somewhere quiet. Like their bedroom, not in the offices of a nightclub.'

'Were there packets of sleeping tablets on her?' Ed asked, washing his tatties down with some milk.

'They were in her handbag. Brand name variety.

Can be bought in any chemist. I called the techs and they're dusting them for fingerprints.'

'Does anybody know about this other man?' Natalie asked.

'We're still trying to trace the girls she was with. The family know who they are, but we don't have any contact details. They were friends of Meghan's, but the family had only met the maid of honour once. We have a man on camera going down to these offices with Meghan, then leaving on his own. We don't know if this was the bloke she was allegedly messing about with.'

'If I was a detective,' Ed said, 'then I would be leaning towards thinking she was murdered. Seems like it was staged. Very clever and very well planned, but not without its flaws.'

'I agree,' Natalie said. 'She killed herself out of guilt?'

'Peter's wealthy,' Ed said. 'She was his only daughter, so she was spoiled. Usually, when some little rich lassie like that messes up, she gets over it. Don't you think?' Ed asked his son.

'In my experience, yes.'

'Unless she was experiencing mental health problems,' Natalie said.

'I spoke to her maid of honour and they'd had a lot of alcohol before Meghan went off with that guy.'

'How likely is it you'll be able to identify him?' Ed asked.

'We don't have a lot to go on. He wasn't looking up at the cameras, kept his head low all the time. But he didn't seem to have a problem getting Meghan away from her friends.'

'Like she knew him,' Natalie said.

'Yes. But they weren't holding on to each other in the way a couple does when they've had too much to drink and like each other a lot.'

'Like you and Chaz,' Ed said, and his son threw him a look. 'What? You two like each other, don't you?'

'I like her a lot more than I like you right now.'

'You don't have to like me, but you have to love me because I'm your father.'

'Let's not put that to the test.'

SIXTEEN

'Why don't you just call me Adam West and be done with it,' Callum had said to his father.

'What?'

'Batman. Duh.'

All the years growing up, Callum never once remembered his father losing his temper, but he had found out that not only did his father occasionally shout, but he had an underlying temper that was usually reserved for people who were so many rungs below him, he didn't know they existed. Until they had to be shouted at.

Now, the ticking bomb exploded. And right in their kitchen too, which would have been bad enough if they'd been alone, but they weren't: the cleaner was in the living room down the hall. Listening to the conversation in between trying to steal the silverware.

'Yes, you bloody well are going to work, my lad!' Father had screamed at him.

Callum had been shocked into silence, wondering if it would be more prudent to run or just stand still and ride it out, like people rode out a hurricane. In fact, he had thought that the weather phenomenon had a lot in common with his father at that moment: fuck with it and you'd die.

'I said, do you understand me?' Father shouted. His face had turned beetroot red, something pulsed in his neck – *a coronary, please God!* – and sweat lined his face like he had been slapped with a wet cloth.

Father had no intention of leaving this world at that moment, and if it was true that the eyes were the windows to the soul, then he was going to burn in hell.

'Yes. Yes, I do. A job. I'll start looking.'

'Will you fuck. You will work in The Dungeon.'

Callum wondered if the cleaner thought they actually had a dungeon, but he knew his father was talking about the pub on George IV Bridge. The building had once been a house of worship, but now it was a different place of worship: crowds of people stood at the altar of Guinness and Tennent's.

That had been six months ago, and Callum had entered the building as an assistant manager. His father had told him he would have been a table cleaner if he hadn't had experience of working in one of the other pubs he owned, so that was always something to be thankful for.

Three months in and the manager, who didn't know who Callum was, had suggested Callum do what he did: pilfer. It was an easy gig, he had said. They could cook the books and make a few quid off it. What do you say?

Callum had spoken two words: 'You're fired.'

The promotion had kicked in the following day and he had to admit he liked being the boss. Not the manager's underling but the real boss. Of course, all the boring stuff was passed on to the new assistant manager, so Callum could spend some time with the women who came into the bar.

Tonight was a washout.

'I'm off, Callum,' Mike, the assistant manager, said, waving as he zipped up his puffer jacket.

'Right, pal, see you tomorrow.' Callum walked to the door with him and saw him out, then closed the door behind him and locked it.

He himself would be leaving shortly. Maybe this working lark had turned him round after all. Father hadn't given him any grief and was pleased with the way he was running things. Not like when he had dropped out of university. He had to admit he had been sailing through life, but this was keeping his feet on the ground. Besides, he got to lie in every morning, just like he was used to.

He switched off most of the lights, keeping on the ones that illuminated his way through to the back office. He turned a corner and stopped dead.

Somebody dressed in black and wearing a pig mask was standing in front of him. Some big bastard.

Callum's breath caught in his throat for a moment, before his feet got the message to run. He turned, and just as the adrenaline hit him, he saw another one, dressed exactly the same as the first.

'Jesus. What do you want? The money? It's in my office. Take anything you want.' He was suddenly sweating and was barely holding on to his bladder.

Then he was roughly pushed from behind, and he fell forward towards the second one, but the short arse one deftly moved out of the way and Callum fell to the floor. He rolled onto his back and put his hands up.

'We want the money, but we want you to stay out of the way so we can get out of here without you calling the police,' the Big Bastard said.

Callum felt relief wash over him. They were robbing the place and that was good. Money could be replaced. 'Take what you want. Help yourself to anything.'

'Good. Don't give us any trouble and you'll be fine. You won't get hurt. Stand up and put your hands behind your back. If you try anything stupid, I'll take the shotgun out of the bag and shoot you dead. Either way, we're taking your money.'

Bag? What bag? Callum didn't see a bag; then he saw the guy lift it from the floor. He must have had it behind him.

Callum got to his feet and saw Short Arse was blocking his way out of here. Better to play along and get out of here in one piece. He turned round and put his hands behind his back. Then he felt a rope going round his wrists and being tied in a knot.

'Get him upstairs,' Short Arse said.

'You heard; move upstairs,' Big Bastard said.

Aw, fuck, Callum thought. *This isn't good.* But he did as he was told. The building had three levels, and they made their way up to the second level, where a balcony ran round from one side to the other, over-looking the bar downstairs.

'I promise I'll sit here quietly –' Callum started to say, but he felt the rope go over his head and tighten on his neck. He screamed and fought for his life, but Big Bastard punched him in the stomach, winding him.

The two people dressed in black turned him round and looked at him as he wheezed.

'This is for Moira. The girl with the glasses. The girl with the speech impediment. The one who didn't fit in with your group. You killed her.'

'I...I...didn't touch...her,' Callum said, trying to catch his breath. He started to pee himself. 'Please. We didn't...mean...it. I didn't...kill...her.' He felt the warm liquid running down his leg.

'She hanged herself and left a note. Remember?'

'She...committed suicide.' He sucked in a deep breath. 'I wasn't responsible.'

'Bullies never are,' Short Arse said, tying the rope to the balustrade. 'Christ, he's pissed himself.'

Big Bastard stepped forward, grabbed hold of Cullum's right leg, and lifted and pushed at the same time. The young man went over the edge.

The screaming stopped.

'Come on, let's go,' he said, grabbing the bag, and they rushed down the stairs.

Short Arse took a jacket off a coat stand and put it on. Big Bastard flicked off the last of the lights, and they opened the door a fraction, peering out. There was no traffic.

They took their masks off and put them in the bag.

Then walked out into the cold, dark night.

SEVENTEEN

Max wasn't just lying at Bracken's feet, he was lying *on* them. He was a very protective dog, and he was quite content to be with Bracken while Ed was eating breakfast.

Bracken was watching the news when Bob came in. 'Mary's worried you've gone off her cooking,' he said.

Bracken smiled. 'Tell Mary her cooking is just fine, Bob. I had a big lunch with Catherine yesterday. We had to have a wee chat about our lassie. I wasn't that hungry afterwards.' If Bob saw through the lie, he didn't say anything.

The truth was, Bracken had a bad feeling in his gut and his appetite had gone out the window. His old DI from Fife, Cameron Robb, was doing a little digging for him.

'You're right to be worried. That Turner laddie sniffing about her. Are you going to have a wee word?' Bob's eyes lit up at the prospect. He too had been on the firearms team who had been in the bank the day Billy Turner was shot and killed.

'I'm reserving judgement,' Bracken answered.

Bob nodded noncommittally. 'You going to grab a piece of toast or something? Mary will bend my ear if you go to work and you haven't had any scran.'

Bracken smiled. 'Aye, a wee bit of toast and a quick coffee.'

'I haven't seen you this eager to get into the office since…well…since never.' Bob laughed and Max looked up as Bracken took his feet back. The German shepherd looked at them both for a moment before putting his head back down.

Bracken's phone dinged. He took it out and read the text. *Coffee?* Chaz.

'Can Chaz come over for a coffee?' he asked Bob, feeling like a ten year old.

'That lassie can come over here anytime, you know that.' Bob tutted as if Bracken knew he didn't have to ask.

'You're like a bloody wee boy,' Ed said, getting wired into some bacon and eggs. 'Chaz is a nice lassie. She can come over here anytime. I won't tell her you're seeing your ex-wife behind her back.'

Bracken looked around the dining room. 'For God's sake. I didn't jump into bed with her. We had a civilised conversation on neutral ground about our daughter. Trust you to make it into something filthy.'

'I'm kidding. You forget your chill pills this morning?'

'I forgot my shot of vodka more like.'

Ed laughed. 'Mind that spoon you worked with down in Leith. He would go to the boozer, then go home and drink a bottle of wine in bed. Like it was something he was proud of.'

'I remember him.' Bracken shook his head and typed a text back to Chaz: *Uncle Bob said you can come round and play. Uncle Ed is here too.*

He got a smiley face in return as he walked over to the packet of Warburton's bread. He popped in two slices and poured a coffee while it was toasting.

'I called Peter Fisher last night,' Ed said. 'He's gutted, as you would expect. He and his wife had to go to the mortuary and identify Meghan.' He shook his head. 'I still don't see that lassie committing suicide.'

'We need to track some of her friends down, but it's hard when we don't have Meghan's phone.'

'I mean, how would you lot know if she'd been force-fed that drink?'

'We wouldn't. If it was done right.'

'That's a bloody disgrace. I hope you find out. But how can you find her friends?'

'There was no sign of her phone. It's not switched on. She might have dropped it or thrown it away if she knew she wouldn't be using it again.'

'This is all too hokey for me,' Ed said as Chaz came in. She had hung her coat in the hall.

'Let me get you a coffee,' Bracken said, standing up and going over to the insulated flasks. His toast had popped, but he had forgotten about it. Now he buttered it, the butter not melting quite as much as it would have had the toast been roasting.

Chaz came up behind him. 'Why don't I just make the coffee while you're being chef there?' she said. 'Top-up?'

'Please.'

She took a flask and poured the coffees. 'What did you get up to last night?' she asked. Their friendship was at a point where they didn't see each other every night. A few times a week was fine for Bracken. He liked Chaz a lot, but sometimes a case got inside his head and he needed to be on his own.

'TV. Reading. What did you do?'

'Caught up with my laundry.'

Bracken realised this was something he had meant to do as well, but he'd forgotten to give Mary the basket. He paid her to do his laundry, like his father did.

They sat back at the table with Ed.

'Let me ask you a question,' the old man said to Chaz. 'Are you ever without your phone?'

'Come on now. I'm a modern woman. Of course not.'

'I thought you were going to ask him if he was daft,' Bracken said. 'I could give you an insight into that.'

'I'm being serious here. Let's not forget my friend's daughter is dead.'

'Sorry, Dad. You're right, of course.'

'Right. So Meghan had her phone on her. We know that, because she texted her mother earlier on in the evening, asking how the dance was coming along at the Watsonians'. Then she just lost it? That I could believe if she hadn't been found dead. Why would she go down to those offices? To have sex with a bloody stranger? No, not Meghan. And her having an affair? Please. Her fiancé is in finance too and they were going to have a great life together. Somebody murdered her. You need to find out who.'

'We're looking into it.'

'You tell him, hen,' Ed said to Chaz. 'Peter told me she had taken tablets and the drink mixed in killed her. How many tablets would it have taken to kill her?'

Chaz looked briefly at Bracken, as if silently asking

permission to carry on. Then she looked at Ed. 'She had around two thousand milligrams of sleeping tablets in her system. Which would have been around forty fifty-milligram tablets. Two boxes, bought over the counter in the chemist.'

'Did they find fingerprints on any boxes?' Ed asked.

'Forensics did,' Bracken confirmed. 'I spoke to them yesterday. Chaz is going to take Meghan's prints today so we can compare them.'

'You don't have to take them,' Ed said. 'They should be on file.'

Bracken sat up a bit straighter. 'How do you mean?'

'She has a criminal record. She killed a wee girl while she was drunk-driving ten years ago. She only got probation, but she almost went to prison. If it hadn't been for Peter, she would have.'

'Money talks, eh?' Bracken said.

'I'm not saying it was the right thing, but he stepped in and she didn't go to prison. If I'm honest, it didn't sit well with me. That lassie knew fine well what she was doing when she got behind the wheel of Peter's car. Just like if she had walked down the street with a loaded gun and it had gone off. She knew what she was doing, even if she was impaired. But she got a slap on the wrist.'

EIGHTEEN

The house was large and modern. Tastefully done, it and its neighbours fitted in quite well on Gamekeeper's Road. Across the road, the old houses were sheltered by high walls and trees. These houses too had walls in front of them, with iron driveway gates. The old, original wall curled round from the dead-end street next to it and seamlessly joined the new one. A double garage was over to one side.

'The key here is, look like you belong here. We're not going to be skulking about like we're going to rob the place. Understand?' Kate sat in the back of the car, feeling the buzz of adrenaline rush through her.

'I understand. We took care of Callum, but I want to finish the job, and leaving this scumbag alive isn't finishing the job.'

Kate's breathing was starting to get faster.

'Take it easy, my love. We're going to fix this problem right now.' William was wearing the same boots as last night. Two sizes too big. Bought in a charity shop for cash.

'I know. I love you. Going to group therapy was the best thing I've ever done.'

'I love you too.' He turned to smile at her. 'Ready?'

'Ready.'

'Right, collar up, hat pulled down and keep looking at the ground. Let's go.'

They stepped out of the warmth of the car and walked up to the driveway, Kate carrying the holdall. It was more of a car park in front of the big house. A red Porsche Cayenne sat in front of the door, a light covering of snow on it.

It was still early, but maybe the man was getting ready for work. William had looked him up last night when he was putting Plan B into action; the man was divorced and it was well known in society circles that he had a string of girlfriends. Was one in there with him now? They were about to find out.

Kate put the bag down at the side, out of sight.

The man answered the door himself, suit trousers and dress shirt on. Getting ready for work, then.

'Can I help you?'

William listened for a second to see if he could

hear a dog, but he thought he probably would have heard it by now.

'Detective Chief Inspector Sean Bracken. Can we come inside? It's about your son.' He moved forward, hoping the man wasn't going to demand to see a warrant card at this point.

Basil Darnley moved to the side as William walked in.

'This is my colleague, DI Sullivan. May we sit down?'

Darnley closed the door and stopped the cold from rushing in any further. 'Go straight ahead.'

They walked through the double doors leading into the living room and turned round to face Darnley. It was a large room with expensive furniture that hadn't been bought from a Swedish store. Everything was high end, and William didn't feel jealousy but utter disgust.

'What's the stupid bastard done now?' Darnley asked.

'He's gone and got himself killed, hasn't he?' Kate shook her head and tutted.

'What are you talking about?' Darnley's face looked halfway between a deflated football and a *Spitting Image* puppet.

'I'm sure your grasp of the English language is good enough to understand what I'm telling you, but just in case you're having difficulty, let me explain in layman's terms: Callum popped his clogs last night. Went right over the balcony in The Dungeon. Whee, just like that, with a rope round his neck.' William made a motion to illustrate his point.

'Who the fuck are you? You're not polis, are you?' Darnley was snarling now. 'I'll have your knees broken.'

'Tsk, tsk. That's a violent streak you have there.' William punched Darnley hard in the guts, winding him. For a few seconds, the man couldn't breathe, and William nodded for Kate to go and get the bag.

She went to the front door and brought it in, some snow falling from it from underneath. She laid it down on the carpet, opened it, brought the boots out and put them below the coat rack. Then she took a rope out of the bag and moved to stand behind Darnley.

'Get out. Or else I won't call the cops – I'll have somebody take care of you,' Darnley wheezed.

William smiled and chuckled. 'Dear oh dear, you are getting a bit excited. But how are you going to have us sorted when you don't even know who we are?'

'You pair of sick bastards.' Only then did Darnley realise that Kate was behind him, and as he turned to face her, she punched him in the stomach.

William took a small rope out and got Darnley's

hands behind his back, the older man struggling but not hard enough to stop what was going on.

William tied the rope round Darnley's hands and began hauling him backwards towards the hallway. Kate followed him, holding the other, longer rope. Darnley was struggling more now, but he was no match for William, who began dragging him up the stairs.

At the top of the landing, Kate put the rope round Darnley's neck and he struggled even more. Kate tied the other end of the rope to the bannister railing, and with the rope pulled tight around the man's neck, William lifted Darnley and pushed him over the edge.

There was a short yell before the rope tightened and Darnley started swinging back and forth like a pendulum.

'Let's go,' William said, and Kate smiled as she grabbed the bag and they made their way out.

NINETEEN

Bracken had Sullivan pull up Meghan Fisher's case file from ten years ago. He sat at the screen and read the story. Seventeen-year-old Meghan Fisher had been at a party in Penicuik. She had driven there in her car and had planned to leave it there, but the last bus had gone and a taxi couldn't come for an hour, and so she had driven home with three friends. She had hit another car after losing control and a five-year-old girl in the other car had died from her injuries.

'Jimmy, get a copy of those prints on file over to forensics so they can compare anything they find on the sleeping tablet boxes.'

'I'll get right on that.'

Bracken's phone rang.

'Sean, it's me, Kara.'

I did see your name, ma'am, he was going to say, but he let it slide. 'Morning.'

'It started out as a good morning, but now things have taken a turn. Get your team over to The Dungeon on George IV Bridge. They've found a body.'

More snow was falling and the roads were all going to hell. Bracken skidded his car to a halt outside the pub.

'Bastard thing's trying to kill me,' he said to Sullivan as they got out into the freezing air.

Patrol vehicles were outside the pub with their flashers on. An ambulance sat further along, as did the mortuary van, as if they were competing for custom.

'Maybe a four-by-four next time for you, sir,' Sullivan said.

'Chelsea tractor? Or maybe one of those wee Japanese numbers that have all-wheel drive and rip your brains out with the G-force.'

'Hardly,' Sullivan said, and he took a tumble as his right leg went out from under him. 'Christ, look at the knee on my trousers.'

'Just count yourself lucky you didn't pull me down with you, or your knee wouldn't be the only part that hurts.'

A uniform was guarding the doorway and nodded

to them as they entered. There was a small crowd in the centre of the large bar. Bracken could see the remnants of a rope still hanging and a white sheet covering the deceased on the floor.

Dr Pamela Green was there, with Chaz by her side.

'Good morning, Sean,' Pam said. 'Come and have a look at what we found when we got here. Although he wasn't on the floor, but rather...' She nodded upwards at the piece of rope. 'We had to cut him down. Although when I say *we*, I mean the forensics crew.'

'Suicide?' Bracken asked.

'I'm not sure yet. His wrists were tied behind his back and I'll be having a closer look at that.'

A man in a white suit leaned over the railing upstairs and shouted down to him, whilst holding a camera and trying not to be added to the tally of dead people in the room.

'Sir? Can you come up here for a minute? And can you put shoe covers on?'

A forensics team member gave Bracken and Sullivan the shoe covers, which they slipped on, then Bracken looked around for a way to get upstairs. He suspected the man in the white suit hadn't had to climb up the rope the corpse had been hanging on.

'Over there,' Chaz said, nodding to a place behind

him, like she was an expert on how to get around in here.

He looked round and saw the stairs through a doorway. He took Sullivan up and they approached the forensics tech, but the man put a hand out to stop them.

'What've you got?' Bracken asked, hoping he wasn't going to be told this was where the guy had jumped from.

'There's piss on the floor,' the man said instead.

'Are you sure it's piss?'

'If it looks like piss and smells like piss and...'

Don't say, and tastes like piss.

'...and passes the litmus test for piss with flying colours, then it's piss.'

'He pissed himself before throwing himself over?' Sullivan said.

'And there's where the puzzle begins. There's a footprint in it. Well, not in the puddle, but it looks like a boot stepped into it before stepping back out and leaving a nice, dry front half of a boot-print. Couple of them, but fading as they get towards you. And no, they don't match the footwear on the victim.'

Bracken looked at Sullivan. 'It's either an assisted suicide or it's murder.'

'The doc has been looking at the rope around his wrists, which are tied behind his back, and in my humble opinion you'd have to be Houdini to tie those knots,' the tech said.

'Houdini used to untie things,' Bracken said.

'Pish posh. You know what I mean. And even if he'd somehow managed to get the rope on in front of himself and then slip his tied hands over his feet, then...well, let's just say I'm a scientist. His wrists are tight together. I mean, I wouldn't bet my house on it, but I'm ninety per cent sure he didn't tie the rope. Plus with the addition of the footprints, I would say that Mr Callum Darnley was helped on his way to the other side.'

'Callum Darnley?' Sullivan said. 'Isn't that Basil Darnley's son?'

'You know him?' Bracken said.

'Only because of what happened seven or eight years ago.'

They all stood in silence for a moment.

'Don't keep us in suspense,' Bracken said.

'Well, we got the report when I was in CID. The mother of a schoolgirl made a complaint against Callum for bullying at school. It was swept under the rug, but he did get a warning from the school. He started his nonsense again, the mother said, and her daughter hanged herself.'

TWENTY

Downstairs, Bracken spoke to Dr Green. 'There are boot-prints upstairs that seem to have stepped in urine. We're treating this as a crime scene for now, unless things prove otherwise. We'll need everybody's shoe- or boot-prints photographed for comparison.'

'If this is murder, Sean, somebody did a good job of making it look like a suicide.'

'That's sometimes the way. When you get him back to the mortuary, could you give me a call? I'll go and talk to the next of kin.'

'Will do.'

'You have a wallet for him?'

'Yes. The address is down in Barnton. One of those big streets with the expensive houses. Seems like it would be too much on a barman's salary,' Pam said.

'Basil Darnley owns this place. He has a string of pubs and clubs,' Sullivan said.

'Does he own Checkers nightclub, where Meghan was found?' asked Bracken.

'I don't know.'

'He does,' Elsie said, holding out her phone. 'I just did a quick Google search.'

'Interesting,' Bracken said. 'Izzie, see if you can get hold of Old Man Basil. I want to speak with him. Don't tell him what it's about. Then when his son is ready for identification, we can take him to the mortuary. Meantime, I want to speak to him face to face. Prepare him for the ID.'

'I'll get right on it.'

Bracken saw Chaz standing off to one side and walked over to her.

'Everything okay?' he said from behind her, and she jumped. She was on her phone and put it away as Bracken approached.

'What? Oh, yes. It's fine.' She forced a smile and Bracken's instinct kicked in. She was far from fine.

'You sure?'

'I'm sure, Sean.' She smiled again and he could see her eyes were glistening. 'Try saying that three times fast. Anyway, how was your lunch yesterday?'

He hesitated for a moment. 'It was with Catherine.

My ex-wife. She works across the road, and we sat down and had a talk about Sarah.'

'Oh. That must have been nice.' Her smile slipped like an old man slipping on ice but managing to correct himself before falling on his arse.

'I just wanted to discuss Sarah's safety –'

'It's okay, you don't have to explain to me. We're just friends with benefits. The benefits being pizza and watching a movie. You honestly don't have to explain yourself to me.' She walked away without turning back.

What just happened? thought Bracken.

TWENTY-ONE

They were an officer down with DS Angie Paton on a course at Tulliallan, and Bracken wasn't sure yet how he felt about Elsie. Her enthusiasm was there, but he was hoping for more spark.

'You think Angie will come back?' Sullivan said as Bracken wondered how good the airbags were. His heart lurched as the back of the car went out, but Sullivan corrected the skid and they were back on the straight and narrow. Whether by chance or skill, Bracken didn't know, but he kept looking ahead and said a little prayer.

'She's supposed to be back, but I think she might divert off to another branch. She's too good to be stuck at sergeant level in MIT. She could work her way up in another department. She's a great critical thinker.'

'Critical thinker,' Sullivan said. 'No, that's wrong.'

'No, that's right, son.'

'Oh, no, boss, I wasn't thinking that. I was thinking of that rhyme about a pheasant plucker. You know, the one you try to say fast?'

'Jesus, where does your heid go at times? And watch that fucking bus.'

Sullivan chuckled to himself. 'My wife's a pheasant plucker.' He looked at Bracken. 'How does the rest of it go?'

'Stop talking.' Bracken had always been a nervous passenger and now was no different. Why he had relinquished control he had no idea, but he would be swapping seats later. Sullivan had commented that Bracken taking over the driving was like swapping deckchairs on the *Titanic*. Cheeky bastard.

Gamekeeper's Road was a street in Barnton, very affluent, with neighbours who didn't leave car parts on their immaculate lawns or whistle out of their windows when the polis entered the street.

'Slow it down, son. I know my eyesight's good, but it's not that good.'

Bracken was looking for numbers. He saw new-builds on the right and then the correct house number came up. 'Over there. With the fancy German car in the driveway.'

'You should get one of those, boss. Better than driving about in this shopping trolley.'

'How much money do you think I earn, exactly?'

'More than me.'

Sullivan pulled the car over on the other side of the road and they got out. Bracken thought this must be what passengers felt like getting off a plane in Antarctica for the first time.

Then he stopped. 'Jimmy, look. The front door's open.'

'Not something I imagine he would do on purpose,' Sullivan said, taking out his extendable baton.

Bracken walked up the snow-covered drive and looked at the footprints there. He was about to tell Sullivan to avoid them, but the DI didn't need his granny telling him how to suck eggs.

Bracken nudged the door open with a boot, feeling the kick of adrenaline. He opened the door wider and saw Darnley hanging in the hallway from the landing above.

Bracken turned to Sullivan and was about to tell him to call it in when they both heard the noise from upstairs.

According to protocol, one should make the call for backup, instead of them both going straight up to investigate. Better that control knew where they were. Sullivan called it in while Bracken watched his back.

Then Bracken led the charge, which meant carefully moving towards the stairs. He couldn't see up the staircase to the upstairs level, so he approached with caution. He could hear Sullivan talking in a muted voice before the DI joined him.

'Maybe it's a survivor,' Sullivan said.

'Or a killer.'

Bracken's wife had always said his glass was half empty all the time. If they were approaching a railway station and two men were walking towards it, Catherine would think they were travellers, whereas Bracken would assume they were muggers. The half-empty approach had served him well and he'd never been mugged.

At the top of the stairs, the landing went round in a horseshoe shape.

'Stay here, Jimmy. I'll check the rooms.'

Sullivan nodded. This way, nobody could come out of a room and make an escape or rush them.

The first room on the right was a bedroom. Bracken walked in, his baton over his shoulder. He flung open a closet door and saw only clothes. He turned back to the room and saw the bed was practically on the floor, so there was no hiding room underneath.

On the landing again, he was about to go into the next room when they both heard a noise coming from a room along the other end.

This, Bracken assumed, was the master bedroom,

as it had double doors. He turned the handle on one and it swung open.

There was a huge four-poster bed against the middle of the back wall. It looked like the Scottish Olympic trampoline squad could practise on it. There were several doors, presumably leading to an en-suite and maybe a couple of dressing rooms. Or maybe to another dimension if this was *The Twilight Zone.*

Bracken turned a door handle as Sullivan guarded the exit.

It was a walk-in wardrobe and there was a young woman standing there looking at him.

'Please. You don't hurt me,' she said in what sounded like a Polish accent.

'I'm not going to hurt you,' Bracken said, running his eyes over her: no sign of blood, she was wearing trainers, not heavy boots, and there was no sign of a weapon.

'Who...who are you? Please don't hurt me. I won't tell.'

'I'm DCI Sean Bracken. I'm –'

She let out the most soul-wrenching scream Bracken had heard in a long time, just before the first patrol car arrived.

Then she passed out.

TWENTY-TWO

The woman was sitting in another room with a blanket round her when Chaz and Pam turned up.

'I heard you had that effect on women,' Pam said to Bracken.

'Thanks, Doc. But I do alright, I'll have you know.'

Chaz was standing back from him a bit and he was expecting another wisecrack to come out of her mouth, but nothing.

'You okay there?' he asked her.

She looked at him as if he'd asked her to solve a riddle, then she snapped out of it. 'What? Oh, yes, I'm fine.'

She didn't look fine, but he didn't push it.

'What happened with the woman?' Pam asked, her tone serious now.

'She started getting hysterical, thinking Jimmy and I were going to harm her. DSup Page is talking to her now, and she told me the woman thinks we killed her boss. She's a cleaner here and was upstairs when two people came in. That was about half an hour before we got here. She was hiding upstairs and didn't want to come out.'

'Jeez, that must have been rough for the poor woman.'

'I don't think she's entirely convinced we're the good guys.'

'What would make her think that?' Pam asked.

'Because the man who killed Darnley used our names.'

'Why would he do that?'

'To gain entry.' Bracken looked down at Darnley as if the dead man had the answers. He probably did, but he was unable to convey them.

'How do they know your names?' Chaz said.

Bracken looked at her again. She was pale and her eyes were bloodshot, as if she hadn't slept well. He couldn't blame her after what had happened before Christmas, when she and some others had been abducted and come close to being murdered. Now one of the abductors was dead and the other one was in Carstairs state hospital.

He stepped closer to her. 'You okay? You don't look well.'

'I'm sorry, I just have a bad headache.'

This wasn't the Chaz he had come to know and have some fun with. She was his friend, and if there was something wrong, he wanted to know about it.

She walked away before he could question her further. This had to be more than her feeling put out by a stupid lunch with his ex-wife. His detective mode kicked in now and he knew something more was wrong, but he left it for now.

Kara Page came across to him and Sullivan. 'Where were you both an hour ago?' she asked bluntly.

'Really, ma'am?' Bracken said.

'You know how it goes. The cleaner heard your names, so how would she know you both? Where were you?'

'At the station. With you.'

She turned to Sullivan. 'And you?'

'With you. At the station.'

'Right then. Interview over, and I can confirm you were with me. Stupid bloody rules, but the PF can't argue with that. Now we have two imposters going about pretending to be you two. But there's one big difference: one is a woman.'

Bracken and Sullivan looked at each other. Bracken thought Sullivan was about to say, *Don't look at me; you're the one who was dancing with his dad*, but neither said anything.

'We have to figure out how they know you, or if they've seen your names in the papers. I'll have somebody go through newspaper articles about your recent cases.'

Izzie came into the room, snow still on her hair. 'I have the door-to-door going on, but considering the properties next door and across the street are large and not close, it's going to take a little while.'

'Good job, Izzie,' Bracken said. 'The footprints leading into the house have been preserved as best as possible and photos have been taken. I want a comparison taken with the boot-print that was found in the pub.'

'I'll get on it,' she said, turning away.

The heat from the central heating was competing with the cold flowing in through the front door.

'The ambulance crew are going to be taking the cleaner away just now. Maybe you and Sullivan could make yourselves scarce,' Kara said.

The detectives walked through to the kitchen.

'Who the hell would want to use our names?' Sullivan asked.

'Somebody with a personal grudge,' Bracken answered.

'Somebody who knows us and wants to get back at us,' Sullivan agreed.

Bracken leaned back against the counter. 'If that was the case, then when they killed Darnley, only he would be the one who knew. Unless they knew the cleaner was in the house and they said it for her benefit too.'

'Bit risky that, boss, don't you think? They might have figured she would call treble nine right away.'

'Yet she didn't. Have her background checked out. Maybe she was just shit scared and hid and couldn't bring herself to call the police, but even people who are petrified and hiding in a closet have called it in. See if she has any skeletons in her own closet, as it were.'

Kara came through to get them. 'The cleaner said Darnley lived with his son. His wife was dead. He didn't have anybody round to the house when she was here, which was every weekday.'

'We should talk to somebody in his offices, but I'm thinking somebody targeted them both,' Sullivan said.

'That would make sense.' Kara looked at them.

Bracken said, 'Look at the chain of events. Meghan was killed in the club. Callum was hanged last night at the pub. His father was killed this morning. Basil Darnley owned both establishments. There's just something there that's not fitting in properly.'

'Go and talk to his office staff,' Kara said to Sullivan. 'Take Elsie with you.'

'I'll get an address from Izzie.'

Kara turned to Bracken. 'We'll get the incident room set up. We can leave forensics here. Let's get everybody up to the station.' She blew out a breath. 'I wish to Christ Angie was here.'

'We'll get by.'

TWENTY-THREE

'What are you doing here?' Sarah Bracken stood looking at the young man on her doorstep, feeling a mixture of anger and excitement.

Mark Turner brought out a bunch of flowers from behind his back and put a stupid grin on his face. 'I am so sorry. I was being a dick. Please forgive me.'

He thrust the flowers out to her.

'Yes, you were. I thought you were scared of my dad or something.'

'I was. He's a big man. He could flatten me with one hand. I was intimidated by him. I ran away like a wee boy. This is a peace offering.'

Sarah wasn't a teenager anymore, but right then she felt like one. Her heart was beating faster and she felt like she was doing something wrong, going behind her dad's back. But this was her own place. She was on a week's break from uni, even though it was only January, and if she wanted some fun, then her dad could go jump.

'Come in,' she said, taking the bunch of flowers. He smiled and she shut the door behind her. 'You know where the living room is.'

He walked through and stood in the middle of the room, looking around awkwardly.

'Have a seat. I'll get a vase for these. Coffee?'

'That would be great. Thanks.'

He took his jacket off as she left the room. Sarah felt excited. Seeing Mark as a friend had been good, but when he had asked to be her boyfriend, she'd readily agreed. She hadn't told her dad that they were actually dating. Although she was old enough, she felt like she needed his approval. It was something she put down to being a copper's daughter.

She fished out her one and only vase from under the sink, put water in it and put in the flowers. Then she switched the kettle on.

'Have you missed me?' Mark said from the doorway and she jumped a little.

'Jesus, you scared me.' She turned and smiled at him.

'Sorry. I'm just so glad that you want us to talk again. I want a second chance, but only if you do.'

'We can certainly talk about it.'

'I'd like that. Here, let me make the coffee. It's not just a woman's job.' He smiled back at her and she laughed.

'Okay. You know where everything is.' She left the kitchen, smelling the flowers once again. 'What kind are they?' she asked from the living room.

'Hand-picked from a hillside in France and imported especially for you.'

She laughed. 'And here's me thinking that you just popped into a petrol station for them.'

'Are you calling me cheap?' he said, laughing.

The kettle boiled and he poured the coffees.

Sarah was still arranging the flowers when he brought her mug in. 'Milk, no sugar, because you're sweet enough.'

'You remembered. How sweet. If you'll pardon the pun.'

He sat down on the settee, putting the two mugs on the coffee table in front of him. The TV was on. Some mindless talk show where the guests were wearing suits that were normally reserved for court appearances.

Sarah tuned it out. She was going to text her dad. Not for permission but to tell him she was a big girl now and had made a big girl decision.

Mark came round. We're going to start seeing each other again. I think you're worried about nothing. He's a nice guy.

She hit send and sat down beside Mark and drank some of her coffee. 'I'm so glad you came round. I was missing you.'

Which was mostly true. Her mood had swung between *I wish he was here* and *I hate that bastard.*

'I was missing you too. I just had to pluck up the courage to come and see you. So, have you thought any more about us seeing each other?'

Sarah laughed. 'You only asked me five minutes ago.' She drank more of the coffee. He had put in a lot of milk, but she didn't want to criticise. It was just easier to drink.

'I know. Honestly, I've never felt this way about anybody in my life.'

They chatted for a few minutes, but Mark's voice was getting lower and lower.

There was another knock at her front door, but she couldn't get up off the settee to answer it. She watched as Mark got up and left the room. What the hell was happening? She felt the room spin.

Then Mark was back. With another man, and they were dragging something in. It was long and black. With a zip up the front.

'Sorry. You won't feel any discomfort, I promise you. You'll be asleep in a minute,' Mark said.

He was out of focus now, and the other man

roughly pushed the coffee table away and they both lifted her up. She couldn't resist.

'It will be a few minutes and then she'll be fully under,' Mark said to his friend as they laid her down on the black plastic. She felt her arms being laid by her sides, then the room started to go dark.

The last thing she heard was the body bag being zipped back up.

TWENTY-FOUR

Bracken was standing in front of the whiteboard. There were a couple of bodies in from CID. One was a grizzled older boy who looked like he could rent himself out as a hot-air balloon at the weekends. His name was DS Tam Gale, which Bracken thought was fitting, because he'd heard that Gale was full of piss and wind. What the hell he was doing here, he didn't know. He could always be sent for a cup of tea. The other one was younger. DC Docherty Lennox. *Call me Doc*, he had said.

'This is what we have so far. Meghan Fisher was found dead yesterday morning in the offices of Checkers nightclub. She was last seen going downstairs from the club with a tall man and only he came back up. There were sleeping pills in her system and enough alcohol to kill her without the tablets.'

'We're thinking she was murdered then?' Gale said, interrupting.

'I'm thinking that, aye,' Bracken said. 'This morning, we found Callum Darnley dead in the pub where he was a manager. We think he was murdered too. We went to inform his father and we discovered him murdered. He was hanged, just like his son. There are a couple of connections. Basil Darnley, the father, owned both premises where Meghan and Callum were found. All of their deaths were made to look like suicide. But that's not all: both Meghan and Callum, directly or indirectly, caused the death of somebody else years ago.'

'Somebody out for revenge?' Doc asked.

'We're working out who those previous victims were and we're tracing their families.'

Izzie looked up from her computer. 'Sir? In the Meghan Fisher case, the little girl in the other car who died was Kirsty Watkins.'

'Good. Find an address for the family. See if they still live in the area. And look up the incident of a young girl hanging herself after being bullied.'

'I already did. I found the police report. Ten years ago, Moira Lamb was being bullied at school.'

'Was it a private school?' Doc asked.

'No. It was a regular high school.' She told them the name.

'I'm surprised,' Bracken said. 'I thought a spoiled wee sod would have gone to a rich boys' school.'

'His father must have been one of the old school,' Kara said. 'You know, send the boy to a regular high school and toughen him up instead of putting a silver spoon in his mouth.'

'Normal high school didn't do me any harm,' Gale said, tugging his trousers up a bit.

'That's why you're the poster boy for CID,' Bracken said.

'Thank you. I think.'

Bracken gave a little shake of his head. Then looked back at Izzie. 'Can you find the address for the family of Moira Lamb?'

Izzie smiled and Bracken put up a hand. 'Don't tell me; you've already found it.'

'I have. The thing is, there's no mention of Callum Darnley in the report. It just says the boy's name was sealed in court papers.'

'That's the only story of a girl hanging herself after being bullied?' Bracken asked.

'It is.'

'It's a good place to start.'

'Terrific,' Kara said. 'Two teams. Go and find the families and find out more. It might be nothing, but we've got nothing else to go on just now.'

'I'll go with you,' Gale said to Izzie.

'Sorry, pal. You're coming with me,' Bracken said. 'Doc, you go with Izzie.'

'Suit yourself, squire,' Gale said.

'That's okay, sir. DS Gale and I can get to know each other a little better.' The smile Izzie gave Gale made Bracken laugh inside.

'Go ahead.'

As Bracken grabbed his coat, his phone dinged. He took it out and read the text from his daughter.

'Oh, Christ, no,' he said.

'Everything okay?' Kara asked as the others busied themselves getting ready to go out.

'My daughter making stupid decisions,' he said.

TWENTY-FIVE

The drive out to Corstorphine was a twenty-minute affair in which Bracken got to know Doc a little bit better.

'How're you liking CID, son?'

'I'm enjoying it, sir. I was in uniform for four years before deciding I wanted to be a detective.'

'You can thank DSup Page for giving you this chance in MIT. We're short of bodies just now.'

'I appreciate the experience. I've been in CID for three years. I'm looking to make my way up.'

'Try to make an impression. It will be good for you in the future.'

Bracken took his phone out and sent a text to Catherine. *Try to talk some sense into our daughter. She said she's going out with that Turner laddie. He's bad news.*

He held on to his phone, looking at the screen, willing it to jump into life. They were going round the Drumbrae Roundabout when it kicked back.

I sent a text to her already this morning, but she hasn't answered. I'll send another one and pass on your best wishes.

'Come on, Catherine, take it seriously for God's sake.'

Doc looked over at him. 'Sorry, sir?'

'Oh, nothing. Women problems.' Bracken looked at the young DC. 'You married?'

'Me? No. I have a girlfriend, though.'

They turned into Craigs Road and stopped on the left by a row of linked houses.

'That one there,' Bracken said, checking his phone. Izzie had sent the address to him and he'd convinced himself it wasn't because he would forget it.

Diane Watkins answered the door, which meant they didn't have to go traipsing about looking for her or come back at God knows what hour. They held up their warrant cards.

'Mrs Watkins?'

'Yes, that's me. Is anything wrong?'

'Can we come in and have a word with you for a moment?'

She stepped aside and let them in, then showed them through to an immaculate living room. Bracken looked at a sideboard over to one side that held photos. A few were of a little girl.

'Can we sit down?' he asked, and Diane nodded, then sat down opposite them. There was no other sound in the house, no TV or radio playing.

'Is your husband around?' Bracken asked.

Diane shook her head. 'No. We're divorced. It's just me now.' She was in her late forties, Bracken knew from the file.

'What's this about?'

'You had a daughter, Kirsty?'

'Yes, I did. She's been gone for a long time now. Is it about her?'

'In a way. Can you tell me a little bit about what happened? I know it's painful, but it would help us.'

Diane looked at him for a moment, then stared past him as if looking at a video of the past.

'My ex-husband had been at the pub. He was drinking up at Juniper Green. I would drop him off there because his pal lived nearby. This particular night, he was more pissed than usual and he had run out of money. They sometimes had a lock-in at the pub. He called me asking if I could come and pick him up. He guilted me into going up there.

'I got Kirsty out of bed and we drove up. I was making the turn from Wester Hailes Road onto Lanark Road. The light had changed to green, so it was my right of way. But as I made the turn, this silly young bitch came firing through on a red, smashing into the side of my car. The back took the brunt of it. Kirsty was killed instantly. I was knocked unconscious and had some cuts from flying glass, but was okay otherwise. The girl who was driving was drunk.'

'I read the report. She didn't go to jail, but got off with a fine and a ban.'

Diane curled her lip. 'Daddy had money. She should have spent time behind bars, but she got away with it. Bitch.'

'Meghan Fisher,' Bracken said.

'That's her. Selfish little cow.' Diane looked at him. 'Why are you asking about all of this now?'

'Did you see the news over the weekend?' Bracken asked. Doc was taking notes, not sure if he should jump in or not.

'What news? I don't watch the news anymore.'

'She died of an overdose in a club. We're treating it as suspicious.'

Diane laughed. 'She's dead? That's the best fucking news I've had in a very long time.'

'I need to ask you where you were on Saturday night. Just a formality.'

'I was here. Alone. Like every weekend. It's what I like. Why?'

'We think she was murdered,' Bracken said.

She looked at him and smiled. 'Ah. You think I killed her? Don't think that I didn't think about it for a very long time. I wished her a very painful death. I would dream about it, I would imagine it when I was walking round Tesco, wondering how I would react if I bumped into her. Would I stove her head in with a tin of beans? Smash a wine bottle and ram it into her throat? I thought that one would have been appropriate. For years, I dreamt she would drive into a wall at a hundred miles an hour, pished out of her skull, and die in a fucking fireball. And you know what I did about it?'

Both men sat silently, and Bracken wondered if Doc was as ready as he was if this woman decided to launch herself at them. In the end, Diane stayed seated and nobody moved.

'Fuck all. I did sweet FA about it. You know why?'

Once again, both detectives were at a disadvantage in this game.

'Because of Kirsty! That's why. If I did something stupid, I would go to prison, and knowing those toffs, I would go away for life. I wouldn't be able to see my little girl's grave again. I go every week. I talk to her like she's still here and I cry. Every single time. That's why I didn't touch that lassie. Not because I didn't want to, but because of my little girl.'

And then Diane broke down. Bracken went over

and sat on the arm of the chair and put an arm around her shoulders. He couldn't imagine how he'd react if somebody touched his little girl. Which made him think of Mark Turner. He would make a phone call to his old DI, Cameron Robb, and chew the fat with him. He was a good guy.

After a little bit of time, Diane stopped sobbing and wiped her eyes with her sleeve. Bracken went back to his chair.

'Sorry. I still get emotional.'

'No need to apologise, Mrs Watkins.'

Her head snapped round. 'I'm Mrs Watkins in name only. I divorced him not long after. If he hadn't gone out that night, our little girl would have been in high school right now, just along the road. Instead, she's in a hole in the ground. Where I hope that bastard is.' She looked at Bracken. 'He couldn't even stick at going to alcohol abuse counselling. I told him I'd divorce him if he didn't go, and he did go. For a little while.'

'Who did he see about his drinking problem?'

'Robert Marshall. Then we went to grief counselling. But that didn't work for him either.'

'Who did you see about that?'

She looked at him before answering. 'Ailsa Connolly.'

They were silent for a moment.

'When's the last time you saw him?' Doc asked. 'Your husband?'

'Years ago. Eight, maybe.'

'Do you know where he is?' Bracken asked.

'No. Once the divorce was finalised, William and I never saw each other again. I think he sent me a birthday card once, but I sent it back. I mean, I loved him. Once. But I loved my little girl more than anything. She was a part of me. I needed her more than I needed him.'

'Do you have an address for him?'

'No. I didn't memorise his address. I just wrote "return to sender" on the card and posted it. I could have burned it, but I wanted to send a message to him. And that was the last time I heard from William Watkins. Even saying his name makes me want to puke. I only kept his name because it's still our little girl's name.'

'What about social media?' Doc asked.

'Like Facebook? Are you kidding me? He can hardly operate a real book, never mind Facebook.'

Bracken stood up and Doc followed suit.

'Thank you for your time. I'm sorry this brought back some dark memories, but you understand why we have to ask.'

'I do. I didn't mean to...you know...'

Bracken knew.

TWENTY-SIX

'We can stop off at a bakery if you like,' Tam Gale said to Izzie, patting his ample gut.

'I've already eaten my lunch,' Izzie answered, driving through Slateford.

'There's a nice wee bakery there. I could fair kill a couple of pies. Come on, Izzie, please. I'm at your mercy. I'm begging you, please. I'm a bear when I'm hungry. I'll respect you for evermore.'

'As opposed to not respecting me if I don't stop.'

'Nah, either way, you're the boss. I'm just winging it until they give me the heave-ho.'

Izzie looked at him and he was giving her puppy dog eyes.

'Oh, for goodness' sake.' She pulled into the side of the road outside the bakery.

Gale beamed a smile at her. 'You're a star, Iz. Can I get you a pie?'

'Aye, go on then. A little bit of something hot inside me won't go amiss.'

Gale grinned at her.

'Don't even, Tam.'

'I said nowt. One pie coming right up. Coke or water to wash it down?'

'Yuck. You ever tried washing down a pie with water? It leaves your mouth greasy.'

'Do I look like a man who drinks water?'

'That's true.'

'Hey, hey, we'll have enough of that talk. Fatso's still in the room. Have the decency to wait until I leave the car before slagging me off.' Gale opened the door.

'Who am I going to slag you off to?'

'That's why you're the rising star here, Iz, and I'm the old fart coasting along.'

'Well, I didn't really want to say anything...'

'Easy now,' he said, laughing and closing the door.

Izzie had been prepared to hate Gale, but she could sense underneath that he was easy-going, and although he wouldn't be promoted to one of the chief's assistants, he seemed to be honest, if not quite as PC as others would like him to be. He was a bit overweight but not colossal. She suspected a decent diet and some exercise would get him back in shape.

A few minutes later, Gale returned with a brown bag and a bottle of Coke sticking out of his pocket, snow covering his hair. He plonked himself onto the passenger seat, rocking the car dangerously and putting the manufacturer's weight warning to the test. He slammed the door and wiped the snow off his hair and onto the dashboard and floor.

'Not my favourite time of year, Iz,' he said.

Izzie was about to tell him to stop shortening her name, but she didn't think it would work. She accepted the pie instead.

'How much do I owe you?' she asked.

'You're alright,' he told her, taking a chunk out of the first pie. 'Luckily for me they know me in there and throw in a bunch of extra napkins,' he said, grinning. 'I've never had pie grease down my shirt yet and I don't intend to start now.'

'Where are you normally based?' Izzie asked.

'Leith. Bunch of good guys down there. We get on well, but of course I'm the original out of the bunch. Boss says I'm too mouthy to move on, but I'm of the old school, Iz. I say it like it is. I started in the polis before everybody had a bloody camera in their pocket. If they only knew what went on in the good old days.'

'Helps keep us in line, though,' she said, wishing she'd asked him to get a bottle of juice.

He reached into his left pocket and brought out a

second bottle of Coke. 'Call me a mind reader,' he said, passing it over.

'Thanks, Tam. It's not true what they say about you.'

'Oh, believe me, it is.' He laughed and tucked into his second pie.

When they were done, she drove along Slateford Road, under the railway bridge, and took a left into Allan Park. She continued until she found the bungalow, near the footpath that crossed over the Union Canal.

The pathway hadn't been shovelled and Gale had to push the gate a couple of times before they could walk up the path, which they assumed was still under the snow.

'Ten inches deep or ten feet, it's the same result when you fall on your arse,' Gale complained as they trudged up to the front door.

Izzie rang the bell, then hit the knocker a couple of times. They thought nobody was going to answer, but just when they were about to give up, somebody opened the front door.

'Can I help you?' the man asked as they held out their warrant cards.

'Mr Lamb?' Izzie said. 'Derek Lamb?'

'Yes, that's me. What's wrong?'

'Can we come in and speak to you?' Gale said, his

nose already starting to turn red.

'Come away in.'

They walked past him and into the warmth of the hallway.

'I have to go. Talk to you later. Love you too.'

The detectives turned to Lamb and he pointed to an AirPod in his ear.

'My girlfriend,' he said. 'Door on your right.'

They walked in and made sure they were facing him, waiting for him to join them.

'Grab a seat. You two look like you could do with a cup of coffee. I have a wee Keurig machine through there.' He pointed through to the kitchen. The wall had been knocked down to make it open-plan.

Izzie and Gale looked at each other. A slight nod from Gale told her he would indeed like a cup of coffee, and if there were any biscuits involved, he wouldn't read them their rights but would instead devour them.

'Garibaldi alright?' Lamb said, walking through to the kitchen and popping the first pod in.

'Gary who?' Izzie asked.

Gale tilted his head slightly to one side, silently asking if she was being serious or not. 'Biscuits, DS Kahn. Biscuits.'

'Not for us, thanks,' she answered, and then saw

the disappointment on Gale's face. 'You've just had two pies. Your heart will thank me.'

'Okay, Ma.'

They watched as Lamb brewed both cups and held them up. 'Milk and sugar?'

'Just milk, thanks,' Izzie said.

'You're killing me here,' Gale said, and they watched as Lamb opened the big fridge and poured some milk into both small mugs.

'It's only skimmed, I'm afraid,' he said as he put the carton back.

'That's fine,' Izzie said again.

'Shoot me now,' Gale said.

Lamb came back with the mugs and handed them over. 'Please, have a seat.'

The living room was clean and well kept, and Gale thought this was good news. Any sign of it being run as a brothel and they would know they were dealing with a con artist, but no such sign was visible. They sat on either end of a light-brown leather couch. At each end was a little table with coasters, as if Lamb regularly had visitors round.

'Is it about Moira?' Lamb asked. His bonhomie level had slipped a bit, but he was clinging on to the smile like a man with dysentery might cling on to the last toilet roll.

'It is. Why do you ask?' Izzie said, while Gale

looked through to the kitchen to see if there might be a stray Garibaldi going about. In his mind, one was rolling towards him shouting, *Eat me! Eat me!*

'I heard on the radio about Callum Darnley being found hanged in his pub. I just figured that you might be round. Maybe to tell me.'

'Can you tell us a little bit more about what happened to Moira?' Gale said, taking a sip of the coffee.

'We know it's hard,' Izzie said.

Lamb held up a hand. 'It's fine. It was a long time ago. Moira came home from school one day and told me she was being bullied at school. She was thirteen and this joker was sixteen. She said it had been going on for a while. My wife and I went to the headteacher about it.'

'Is your wife home?' Izzie asked.

'No. We divorced a year after Moira's...death. Kate and I fought like cat and dog after that, each of us blaming the other.'

'The headteacher did nothing about it, I assume?' Gale said.

'Oh, he listened right enough. Made all the right sounds, like, *I'll deal with it,* and the like, but he did nothing. It was swept under the carpet. It did die down for a little bit, but it started up again.

'Then one day Kate came home from work and

found Moira hanging by a rope tied round one of the rafters in the attic. When I got home from work, the ambulance crew were here, but there was nothing that could be done. Moira had left a note telling us what had happened. I wanted the police to arrest Callum Darnley, to charge him with something, but in the end his father made sure that nothing happened to him.'

'He and his father are both dead. We're treating their deaths as suspicious,' Izzie said.

'And you think I had something to do with it?'

'We just need to ask you where you were last night,' Izzie said softly.

'To eliminate you from our enquiries,' Gale added.

'When you came in, I was on the phone to my wife, Sharon.'

'You said it was your girlfriend when we came in,' Izzie reminded him.

'I meant wife. Sorry. I moved on from this, so much so that I got married last Saturday. Sharon's away shopping just now, buying some new clothes for our honeymoon. We're not going away until the warmer weather, but she's excited. We were both in last night, looking at videos of New York.'

'We might need to talk to your wife,' Izzie said, 'but where's your ex-wife?'

'I have no idea. Our marriage crumbled after Moira's death. I haven't had contact with her for a very long time. The last time I saw her, we were at grief therapy and I thought everything was going fine, until she stood up, looked at me and said, "I can't do this anymore." Then she walked out. Out of the office, out of my life.'

'Who were you seeing for therapy?'

'Ailsa Connolly.'

Izzie put her mug down on the table. 'Thank you for your time, Mr Lamb. Sorry for your loss.' She stood up, and Lamb stood up and smiled.

'It was a long time ago. I'll never forget her, but these days I can think about her without crying.'

Gale stood up. 'Thank you for your time.'

Outside, Gale pulled up the collar on his coat. 'You realise I cried a little bit when you said no to the biscuits?'

'Sorry for your loss.' Izzie shook her head and walked back to the car through the deep snow.

TWENTY-SEVEN

'It's a solid building. Old, but very well maintained,' the estate agent told him as she unlocked the front door.

'It looks like a fine old place. We've been looking for something with character but that isn't falling apart.'

'You've found just the right place then,' she said, beaming a smile at him. She flicked the lights on and closed the door behind them. The interior doors just inside were being held open by doorstoppers. 'These can be closed and locked for security,' she said as they entered the main room.

'Good to know.'

'You're a video games developer, my colleague told me,' she said.

'Yes. We're in a house just now. Everything is a bit

cramped now that we're expanding. That's why we're looking for a bigger place to rent. This seems ideal, since the house where we're currently working is in Leith anyway and we know the area.'

'Terrific.'

He looked around the large, open hall. There were outlines where the counters used to be. He was trying to picture it as it had been previously, but he could only use his imagination since he had never set foot in the place before.

'Can we look at the offices?'

'Absolutely. This way.'

He followed her through the back, only half listening to what she was saying as she showed him each of the offices.

'This way to the upstairs.'

They were still in the back corridor and their footsteps echoed on the stone floor as they made their way up to the next level, which was the top floor in the two-storey building. *Two stories AND a basement,* he said to himself, smiling at the woman's back.

She showed him around the other offices, some other rooms and the canteen.

'There's a basement too, I believe?' he said, smiling at her.

'Yes, there is. No lift, I'm afraid. They obviously

had big arms in those days, carrying the goods upstairs from below.'

They walked back into the main hall, and once again their shoes echoed on the stone floor. *Marble,* the man thought.

'This belonged to a shipping company at the turn of the century,' the woman added as they went through another doorway. 'That office through there belonged to the owner of the shipping line. I can picture you sitting there at a desk, writing those...whatever games it is you write.'

Completely out of her fucking depth, he thought but carried on smiling.

'This way to the lower level.'

They went through a heavy door and walked down two flights of stairs to the basement level.

She stopped and smiled at him. 'Here we are. The last rooms in the building. Impressive, aren't they?'

'They are indeed,' Mark Turner said. 'I like what I see. I have one more place to look at, but I'm leaning towards this place. It's absolutely spot on.'

He looked at his watch, hoping that his friend was upstairs by now, hiding.

'I have a meeting shortly, but I would like to thank you for taking the time to show me around,' he said as they made their way back upstairs.

At the door, he held out his hand for her to shake.

'I'll be in touch.' *You'll never fucking hear from me again.*

'I look forward to it.'

They stepped out into the falling snow and the woman locked up behind them.

Locking his friend inside.

TWENTY-EIGHT

'Jesus, it must be freezing up there with all this wind and snow,' William said to Kate as he parked the car. They had pulled in through the site gates and parked off to one side. It was a hard-hat area and they'd brought their own. He looked up to the top of the concrete building, which was just a shell for the moment.

'Damn wind is going to mess up my hair,' Kate complained.

'You look just fine,' William said.

They sat on the front seats and pulled on their welly boots. Not only was it a hard hat area, but there was enough mud to make it a pig-in-shit area.

'You think we did the right thing, don't you?' Kate asked.

'With Basil Darnley?'

'Yes.'

'Of course we did. Look, this is all fine and dandy, like what we're about to do. It's the Big Plan. Well, we deviated from it slightly, because we wanted to. *You* wanted to kill Darnley. I agreed and we carried it out.' He smiled at her in the darkness of the car. 'You don't regret it, do you?'

There was a smile on Kate's face. 'No. He had to die.'

'I agree. We did the right thing,' William said. 'Now, though, we have this pond life to take care of.'

William took the cardboard tube and locked the car and they pulled on their hi-vis vests. The snow had stopped for the moment, but the afternoon light had faded. Their timing was perfect.

They made their way across to the Portakabin, where there were lights on. The men had left for the day and they knew the last man standing would be the man they had come to see.

William walked up the wooden steps outside the cabin and knocked on the door, Kate just behind him.

A young, gruff man answered the door. 'What?' he said.

'Benedict Cuthbert?'

'Aye, that's me. If you're looking for a tour, come back tomorrow,' he said, about to close the door.

'We'll be getting a tour alright, but it will be right now, or else you won't have a job tomorrow.'

Cuthbert wasn't used to being spoken to like that and he opened the door fully. 'Who are you?'

'We're with Mathers and Longhorn. The people financing this project.'

'I know who you lot are.'

William looked at Cuthbert and thought it must have been by the slimmest of margins that Cuthbert had decided to be a contractor instead of the Queen's personal butler.

'We've had word that the computer system of Barclay and Jones, the architects, may have been compromised.'

'Hacked?' Cuthbert asked.

'Exactly. If we find out that *is* the case, then we'll have to shut the whole job down until all the drawings are gone over.'

'Christ, that will mean a lot of men being laid off. This is a bad enough time of year, what with the weather, without some cock messing about with the computers.'

William looked at Kate. 'I have a copy of the plans here that were printed off this afternoon. Maybe we could go up just now to the top floor and compare them while Kate here has a look around. She has a schematic on her iPad that she can look at.'

Cuthbert stood and thought about it for a second. 'If it will save you lot closing down the whole site, let's go.'

Cuthbert grabbed his hard hat and his own cardboard tube and he locked the cabin door behind him, mumbling away to himself while William and Kate stood back down in the mud.

'We have to celebrate tonight,' Kate said in a low voice. 'I think you just won the award for the biggest bullshitter of the year.'

'And how are we going to celebrate?' William replied, smiling. Then, 'Shh. Here he comes.'

The steps to the cabin protested alarmingly as the young man stomped down them like he was at a barn dance.

They walked over the site, wading through snow and mud. There was no attempt at small talk. They entered the concrete and steel shell and walked over to one side, where a construction site elevator was waiting. It was big enough to hold the three of them, and Kate pulled her collar up against the biting wind that was running through the open building.

They got out one floor from the top. Kate and William walked away from Cuthbert.

'Let's get this done and dusted as soon as,' the arrogant young man said. His face was like an overripe plum about to explode.

William walked away towards the edge, while Kate took out a notepad from her pocket and started looking around.

'I thought he said you had an iPad, not a notepad?' Cuthbert said, walking across to her. The wind was screaming into the open-sided building, but Cuthbert didn't seem to notice.

'He lied. But let's go for a walk.'

'A walk. What are you talking about? Are you serious? I think you two are just wasting my time –'

Cuthbert's voice was cut off by the hammer connecting with his knee. He let out a scream that was plucked by the wind and thrown off into the darkness.

Just for good measure, William hit him with it again.

Cuthbert turned round to face him and William hit him in the face with it. Not enough to kill him but to throw him down. Enough to incapacitate him for a moment. Cuthbert fell to the concrete floor.

William dropped the hammer and put his arms under Cuthbert's armpits while Kate got his legs. They carried him over to the edge, Cuthbert struggling.

'This is for Matt Ernestine,' William said.

'Wh...who?' Cuthbert said.

'The student you were at uni with. The one who you dared to walk the edge of the rooftop. The one who fell to his death.'

'I didn't mean it,' Cuthbert gasped, sweat lining his face.

'Well, we mean this, you piece of shit.'

They swung Cuthbert backwards and forwards, the young man trying to grab hold of something, anything, that would save his life, but there was nothing within reach.

Then, suddenly, he was sailing through the dark air. Headlights on cars coming from Glenlockhart were a blur for a few seconds, before he hit a cement mixer below and the dirty orange machine cut his scream short.

William grabbed his hammer, and he and Kate made their way to the elevator. They rode it down, smiling in the dark.

'Success,' William said, and he looked at Kate, falling even more in love with her. But it wasn't love that was making him feel like he was walking on water; it was the urge to kill again.

TWENTY-NINE

It had been a hell of a long day for Bracken. One of those days when you felt like you had got up a week ago and hadn't slept since.

They were in the incident room, heat flowing from the old heaters. He could see the tiredness in his colleagues' eyes. Coming in from the cold into a nice warm office had set them a competition: see which one falls asleep first. To give them their due, each of them was fighting against first prize.

'Izzie, give us a rundown on Moira Lamb's family, please.'

Izzie walked up to the whiteboard and faced the others in the room. 'Moira Lamb's parents divorced shortly after they began grief counselling. Their marriage was destined to fail after their daughter's death. They didn't blame each other, but something broke. Kate Lamb walked out on her husband and they got divorced and he hasn't seen her since.'

Bracken nodded and stepped up beside her. 'We talked to Diane Watkins. She told us pretty much the same thing: her marriage failed after the death of their daughter, Kirsty. Her husband, William, left and he dropped off the face of the planet after sending her a birthday card. She hasn't seen him since. Also, they went to grief counselling too.' He turned to Izzie. 'Do you know who the Lambs saw?'

'Ailsa Connolly.'

He nodded. 'So did the Watkins.' He faced the room. 'This was obviously before Ailsa was arrested. How did it go with Basil Darnley's office staff, Jimmy?'

'Nobody stood out. Darnley was a bad-tempered sod, but he was well liked. Nobody knew of any shady dealings, but then they would say that, wouldn't they? Still, the overall picture was, no one in particular disliked him enough to kill him.'

'There's probably a list bigger than a telephone directory of people who wanted him out of the picture, and that would be the road I'd go down if it weren't for his son being murdered. And Meghan Fisher,' Kara Page said.

'Tomorrow, we should concentrate on finding William Watkins and Kate Lamb. See where they've been spending their time. Meantime...' Bracken picked up a dry-erase marker and drew some lines next to names. 'The only connections we have are Kate Lamb to Callum Darnley, and William Watkins to Meghan Fisher. Parents who lost children to those two people. We need to find them to eliminate them from the enquiry.'

'And let's not forget that maybe one of them went one step further and eliminated Basil Darnley,' Kara said.

'Let's call it a night,' Bracken said.

THIRTY

Bracken had always hated January. Cold, boring and not worth a sook. He would take three months off the calendar if he could and just leave the other three seasons, kicking winter into touch.

Last Christmas had been his best in a while, even though he had almost not survived to see it. Chaz was the best thing that had happened to him in a long time, so he questioned himself as to why he was giving her the runaround.

He didn't have an answer.

What he did have was an empty plate in front of him again. He was sitting across from Kara Page and they had made a pact not to talk shop at the dinner table.

Ed came in. He had insisted that he help clear the dishes and do any washing up that needed to be done in return for Mary and Bob letting Max stay in Ed's room with him. But dinner hadn't been served yet.

'Where's dafty?' Bracken asked.

'Hey, that's no way to talk about Max,' Ed complained.

'I was talking about you,' Bracken replied, nodding to the dog, who was standing just outside the dining room door.

'Aye, that's it, son, keep it up and maybe your boss and I can sit down and have a wee sociable drink in the lounge one night and I can spill the beans about your secrets.'

'Impossible, old man. I don't have any secrets.'

Kara smiled at Ed. 'Thanks for the offer, but I don't think I could handle any more secrets, Ed.'

'Suit yourself, Kara. Just tip me the wink when you change your mind.'

'We're still on for poker later, though, right?' she asked him.

'Although it pains me to take your money, I'm desperate, so yes.'

'You forgot to add, sad and lonely,' Bracken said.

'That would make it sound like a comedy act. Besides, I'm teaching Kara a few pointers.'

'Like, don't play poker with you?' Bracken said.

'Like I said before, just give me a shout when you want me to teach you, son.'

'Better men than you have tried to con me. Your feeble attempts at trying to part me from my money are wasted.'

Ed smiled at Kara. 'You can't blame me for trying.'

Bracken's phone dinged. He took it out. 'Excuse me,' he said to Kara and left the dining room, patting Max on the head as he passed.

In the lounge, Natalie was sitting with Rory while he did his homework.

'Sorry, I didn't mean to disturb you.'

'No, you're fine, Sean. Take a seat if you want.'

He sat down and read the text: *Hi, Dad. Just wanted to say hello. Mark and I are getting on like a house on fire. Please don't worry about me. Love you. Xxx*

He typed back, *Love you too xxx*, then put his phone away. He was still worried about Sarah. Right now, though, he wanted to go and see Chaz.

He got up and left the lounge, and saw Mary coming along the hallway with the dinner plates.

'Are you sure you don't want dinner, Sean?' she said.

Bracken and his wife had gone out as a foursome with Bob and Mary back in the day, but now she clucked about him like a mother hen.

'I'm sure. I'm going to go round and see if Chaz wants to grab a bite.'

'Tell her I said hi.'

He thought about driving round, but the snow had stopped and he didn't want to. He felt like a beer, the car was parked for the night, and if he needed to go somewhere, he could always ask his dad to drive him. That would be like asking a five year old to land a plane, but sometimes you had to just go on a wing and a prayer. He smiled at his own pun.

He crossed over St John's Road, which was still busy but not gridlocked with traffic. He slogged through the fallen snow on the pavement and walked along to Station Road and down to Chaz's apartment block.

He walked into the common stairwell and heard raised voices from above. A man and a woman. Chaz.

He took the steps two at a time and saw a tall man standing at her door.

'Come on, Chaz. Cut me some slack. She kicked me out.'

'So you come all the way up to Edinburgh to find somewhere to crash? Give me a break.'

'No, no, I came up to see my mother. But I can't crash there. Come on, it won't be for long.'

'Danny, we're divorced. I don't have to let you anywhere near me now. Go away.' She tried to close the door, but he put his foot in and stopped it shutting.

Chaz opened the door all the way. 'Get your foot out!'

'Better do as the lady says,' Bracken said, stepping up onto the landing.

Danny smiled. 'I think you'd better mind your own business, old man.'

Bracken approached, keeping his hands in his pockets. Just to give Danny a fighting chance if push came to shove.

'Take your foot out, pal,' Bracken said.

'What's it to you anyway?'

Danny was as tall as Bracken but not as wide. He was younger by a good ten years, but Bracken wasn't worried.

Then Danny took his foot out of the door and took a step towards Bracken.

'I think you'd better leave, son,' Bracken said, taking his hands out of his pockets now.

'Is that right? And why would I want to do that?'

The next move was on Danny. He lifted both arms to shove Bracken.

Bracken had been expecting a punch; a shove had been his second choice. No matter: he was prepared for either.

He sidestepped, pushing Danny's arms out of the way, reached his right arm over and grabbed Danny's head, stepped round him, grabbing the other side of his head with his left hand, kicked his knee out from under him and lowered him to the floor. He could have done it so that Danny landed on his head, but hurting him wasn't the point here.

Bracken let Danny's head go and stepped round, putting a boot on the younger man's chest. 'If I were you, son, I would get up and leave. If you get up and decide you want to take this to the next level, there won't be a next level for you. Understand?' He put more weight on Danny's chest.

'Yes.' Danny tapped Bracken's boot with his hand. Bracken got off him and watched as Danny got to his feet.

'Why are you getting involved?'

'Remember the boyfriend I told you about?' Chaz said.

'Oh, Christ. You're the boyfriend,' Danny said to Bracken.

'Yes, I am. DCI Bracken. That was my version of a handshake. Next time, I'll personally give you a tour of the West End cells. You won't like them.'

Danny dusted himself down. 'So that's a no on the couch, then?'

'That's a no, son.'

'Fair dos. See you around, Chaz.'

'No, Danny. There's no *see you around* anymore.'

Danny walked down the stairs without looking back. They heard the front door close.

'I wasn't very hungry earlier, but now I seem to have worked up an appetite. You fancy something to eat?' Bracken asked.

Chaz stepped aside to let him in. 'Offering to buy me dinner now that you're my boyfriend? You are getting bold.'

'I'll even pay for it.'

'I'm hungry, Sean Bracken, but not for food. Well, maybe food later.' She pulled him in and shut the front door.

THIRTY-ONE

The van didn't handle well in the snow with its rear-wheel drive. There were better vans on the market, but when you were working on a budget, a ratty old Ford was the best you could conjure up and be done with it. Besides, as a makeshift hearse, it was the business.

Mark Turner was impressed by the way he'd handled the tour with the estate agent. Games producer indeed. He was lucky if he could get through a Fortnite game without getting blown away.

He had achieved what he had set out to do, and that was letting his friend come in through the unlocked front door and stay in the place, keeping out of sight.

Now, Turner turned into the little car park of the old building in Leith. One that he had heard many things about over the years, none of them good.

The van skidded to a halt and Turner thought he was going to hit the back wall, but the old van did him proud and stopped in time.

He killed the lights and looked into the back. The bag was still and he hoped that she wasn't dead. If she was? That was a bridge they would have to cross.

The back door of the building opened. He hadn't seen it open at first, which was a good sign. Bellend had remembered to keep the lights off.

The man moved out of the building and came up to the driver's window. 'Everything okay?'

'Fine. Get round the back and I'll unlock it. Let's get inside before some nosey sod comes along and starts to have a neb and wonder what we're up to. I'm sure they use this car park for having a pish on the way home from the pub.'

He jumped out of the driver's side, careful not to break something; it wouldn't look too good here if an ambulance turned up. He slipped round to the back and unlocked one of the van doors and opened the other.

'She's not dead, is she?'

'I don't know, Doctor. You tell me.'

'I'm just asking.'

'Just grab an end, Adam, and we'll get her inside.'

Adam Malone pictured Sarah's father when they had met in the pub last Saturday and hoped Turner was sure of his plan. DCI Sean Bracken was a big bastard.

They lifted the bag through the back door of the old building and shut the door.

The first part of the plan had worked out just fine.

THIRTY-TWO

Bracken sat on the couch, his boots under the coffee table. The TV was on now, but he wasn't paying attention.

'If you'd been running a marathon, I'd have been impressed by your speed,' Chaz said, coming in with two bottles of beer. 'Since you don't smoke,' she said, handing him a bottle and clinking them.

'And that was even with taking time to get my boots off.'

'You never told me you were a sprinter type of man.'

'I'm full of surprises.'

'Yes, you are,' she said, sitting beside him. She gave him a kiss. 'Listen, what I said to Danny about you being my boyfriend, that was just to get him to sod off.'

'I know.'

'Thank you for slipping into the role so easily.'

'I've had some practice over the past few weeks.' He drank some of the cold beer. 'Is that why you had a face on?'

'A face on? That's one way of putting it. But yes, he came up last night too, and tonight was episode two, where the big copper steps in and saves the day. Tune in next week to see if the copper will get his boots off again.'

He looked at her, feeling like he was fifteen again and wanting to ask Rosie if he could shove his hand up her jumper. 'About the boyfriend thing...'

'Yes?'

He could see she was playing it cool, like it wasn't a big deal.

'I mean...would you want to be my girlfriend? If the opportunity arose?'

'If I got you in a raffle, you mean?'

'Oh, Christ, did that sound as bad to you as it did to me?'

'I think it did. It made my ears bleed.'

Bracken drank some more of the beer. His face felt flushed, and it wasn't from the extracurricular activity they'd just taken part in.

'Would you be my girlfriend if I asked you?'

'Are you just putting feelers out here? If I say no, then you'll say, I wasn't asking anyway?'

He laughed. 'I met Catherine when I was eighteen. We got married at twenty. I haven't done this for a long time.'

'You've been divorced for six years. How did you approach all your other girls? How much for ten minutes? Five minutes if I keep my boots on?'

'I had a couple of longer relationships, but we just sort of fell into them. If that makes sense. Other times, it was just me seeing a woman and we went out a few times. No strings attached.'

'Go on, ask me if I want to be your girlfriend,' Chaz said, smiling.

'Chaz, will you be my girlfriend, said twelve-year-old Sean Bracken to the lassie with the pigtails.'

She laughed. 'Sorry, but no, I can't be your girlfriend just now. I'm betrothed to another.'

'I fucking knew it. You're just taking the piss.'

She playfully slapped his arm. 'No, I'm not. Of course I will. If you're asking.'

'I'm asking.'

'I'm dancing.' She leaned over and gave him another kiss.

THIRTY-THREE

'You were late getting in last night,' Ed Bracken said. 'Were you blootered again?'

'Christ, if you're not nebbin at your door, you're chastising me for having a few beers.'

'I was not nebbin. Max growled when he heard you coming in. I'm just making conversation. Can't a dad be concerned about his son?'

Bracken buttered some toast and poured himself a coffee before sitting down. 'Your concern is very touching, but I'm a big laddie now, Dad. Where's Max?'

'In the lounge, chewing on a bone thing I got from the pet shop.' Ed sat down with his own toast. 'Or the couch. God, I hope it's not the couch.'

'You cutting back or something?' Bracken buttered his toast.

'Just trying to watch my figure. I enjoyed that

dancing the other night and my pal and I might go uptown one Friday night.'

'Tell me you're having a laugh.'

'There's life in this old dog yet. But let's not talk about me; let's talk about you. And I'll bet that's a line you've spun many a time.'

'First of all, Grandpa, that is not a line I've spun to anybody. And I have nothing to talk about.'

'Not even Chaz?'

'Well, we made it official last night: she's my girlfriend.'

'That's something we've all known here in the guest house for weeks. I think Bob won the pool.'

'What pool?'

Bob walked into the dining room with another flask of coffee. 'That you wouldn't ask her before last Saturday. Kara had next Saturday. That's going to sting; she was in it for thirty quid.'

'You know what? You're all a shower of –' Bracken was cut off by his phone. It was a text from Catherine. *You heard from Sarah?*

He replied, *Last night. She's fine.*

I don't know if she's angry at me, but I didn't hear from her. L8r.

And that's when it hit Bracken that his daughter might not be fine after all. *L8r.* Short for later. That was something that was missing from Sarah's text. She always wrote in those electronic hieroglyphics. Just like the last time she wrote to him, but it didn't hit him then. Now it did.

Kara came into the dining room, pulling a jacket on.

Ed looked at her. 'Sorry, you lost the pool.'

'Oh, no. Only a few days to go.' She looked at Bracken. 'Congratulations, but we need to go. We'll take your car. Craiglockhart.'

Bracken got up. 'What's happening over there?'

'Dead man on a cement mixer. It's complicated.'

'Where have I heard that before?' Ed said, grinning.

Bracken made a face, took a bite of toast and washed it down with a mouthful of coffee. 'Now I can tell my dad I've had my breakfast.'

The traffic was already giving Edinburgh a kicking, but Bracken used his magic powers, which consisted of flashing lights and a siren. The Police Scotland version of riding a broomstick. They were able to cut down Balgreen at warp speed. Or as fast as the slick roads would allow them.

Luckily, the building site was on the opposite side of the morning rush hour traffic heading into the city and they pulled in across the road behind the other emergency vehicles.

'You remember when this used to be a Land Rover dealership?' Kara asked him as they got out.

'I do,' he answered, looking at the concrete tower and trying to imagine where the cars used to sit. Every little space in Edinburgh was being converted into flats now.

'This is going to be flats, believe it or not,' Kara said.

'I believe it. Princes Street Gardens will be next.'

'It's a hard-hat area, boss,' Tam Gale said, dishing out the yellow hard hats. Bracken was surprised to see the man here so early.

'What do we have, Tam?' Bracken asked.

'The site manager fell off one of the higher levels, it looks like. The pathologist is here already. Forensics have set up a tent around the body. He was already covered by some snow when the uniforms got here.'

'Show us the way,' Kara said.

They walked through snow and the underlying mud. The snow had stopped coming down hours ago, but what had come down was conspiring to make them fall and dislocate something. They saw the tent. Izzie was there, with Sullivan and Elsie.

Bracken and Kara let on to them and entered the tent. It was large, almost like they were going to have a wedding party in it.

Dr Pam Green was there, and Chaz. He smiled at

her, wondering who'd lost their shirt in the mortuary pool.

'Good morning, Kara. Sean,' Pam said to them.

'I was going to ask what we have here, but I can see for myself,' Kara said, looking at the man lying on his back on a tarp next to a cement mixer. 'I'm assuming we're here because something doesn't look quite right?'

'Yes, indeed. It looks like he fell from a great height, and I would say he has at least a broken back and massive internal bleeding. He landed on his back on the mixer and stayed there. We brought him down to examine him and I saw this mark on his forehead.'

Bracken and Kara stepped forward and bent over to have a closer look. There was a round mark in the middle of the man's forehead. They straightened up and looked at the doctor, waiting for her to pull something out of her bag of tricks. Like an explanation.

'Looks like a hammer blow,' Bracken said like a schoolboy who shouts out the answers in class.

'Cigars all round. That's what I would put my money on if this was a betting situation.' Pam gave Chaz a wry smile, but she just shook her head and looked away. 'A hammer blow, probably to stun. If it was meant to kill, it would have gone right into the skull, but that isn't the case here. I would say with certainty that hitting the cement mixer would have killed him, but the exact cause of death, like a bone piercing his heart or something similar, is still to be determined.'

The cement mixer stood silently, mucky and orange and caked with cement scars from campaigns of old.

'There was somebody up there with him and they hit him in the head with a hammer before helping him over the side,' Kara said.

'But that's not all; his kneecap is shattered too. The right one. Most likely the aforementioned hammer coming into contact with it, I would say.'

'Incapacitate him, smack him in the head to disorientate him and then heave him over the side,' Bracken said.

'That's pretty much the size of it. Now we just need the finer details.'

'Thanks, Pam,' Kara said. 'If you could email the preliminary before the full report.'

'Will do.'

Kara and Bracken left the relative warmth of the tent. Warm, as in it wasn't getting smacked by the wind inside.

Sullivan walked over with his notebook in his hand. 'We got an ID from his colleagues. Some of them turned up and found him on the cement mixer. His name is Benedict Cuthbert. He's the site manager for this place, but one of the guys said his father owns the building company itself. Cuthbert Construction. The company that's building these flats.'

'I've heard of the father,' Kara said. 'He rose up from being a small-time contractor to owning half the building sites in the city. He's a big name. Loaded.'

Tam Gale walked up. 'I just spoke to some of the lads and it seems Cuthbert liked a wee swally. Maybe he took a heider from up there.'

'Not with a smashed kneecap and a belt to the forehead with a hammer,' Bracken said.

'Oh. Anyway, he wasn't liked around here. Apparently, Daddy made him work as a site manager so he could keep an eye on Junior in there. Seems young Benedict couldn't keep his eye off a bottle and liked to get behind the wheel when he was blootered.'

'Did he have a record?' Bracken asked.

Gale nodded. 'I asked them and they were only too willing to dish the dirt on him. He was a pisshead who always relied on Daddy to get him out of trouble.'

'Did he kill anybody while he was drunk-driving?'

'Not that they know of. But I was reading the file on Meghan Fisher's arrest. She wasn't the only one in the car at the time; there were three others. Callum Darnley and Benedict Cuthbert were two of them.'

'Who was the other one?'

THIRTY-FOUR

'Caitlin Jordan?'

The young woman who answered the front door was standing there looking puzzled.

'Who are you?'

'Police. I'm Detective Superintendent Kara Page. This is DCI Bracken. Can we come in and talk? It's about your father, I'm afraid.'

'Oh, God. Has something happened to him?' She walked away from the door and the two people walked in behind her, the man closing the door behind them.

'Not yet,' Kate said. She smiled. It never failed to amaze her how people wouldn't ask for ID after you hit them with a shock. Mention that a family member might be in trouble and all defences were lowered as they started to panic.

'What do you mean?' Caitlin started to say, but

Kate was all over her, putting an arm around her neck and clamping a hand over her mouth. Caitlin struggled and kicked, but she hadn't got around to putting her shoes on yet as she was getting dressed for work.

Kate was strong. She worked out in the gym and made sure she did cardio work to keep herself in tiptop condition. Caitlin, on the other hand, arsed a bottle or three of red wine every week, couch-surfing as she caught up with her favourite soaps, in training for her binge-drinking sessions at the weekend with her friends.

Work was a chore, but Daddy insisted, or else he wouldn't help to bale her out when she got herself neck deep in the shit.

Kate manhandled Caitlin through to the bedroom without any help from William, who was only too glad to keep away from the flailing legs. Last time they'd done this, he'd got kicked in the face.

Kate threw Caitlin onto the bed and that was when William jumped into action, knowing what he had to do without being told. He walked into the en-suite bathroom and filled the bathtub with warm water as Kate sat on top of Caitlin. Kate had kept her hand over Caitlin's mouth until she pulled the knife out and held the blade close to her eye.

'You move, you're the one who'll ram your eyeball onto my knife.'

It was enough to stop Caitlin struggling.

'Scream one time and I'll ram the knife into your brain. Got it?'

Caitlin got it but couldn't convey the message because of the close proximity of the shiny blade. They locked eyes and Kate knew the other woman had got it.

William came back into the room. 'Trust me, I get no pleasure from this,' he said as he and Kate started stripping Caitlin. More struggling, but a hard slap from Kate stunned her for a few precious seconds. They dragged the now-naked Caitlin into her bathroom and lifted her into the bath.

William left the room for a moment before returning.

'Sit down and shut up,' Kate said.

Caitlin was crying and covering her modesty. 'Why are you doing this?'

'You know why, honey. You play with fire, you get burned.'

'What does that even mean?'

'It means not even your daddy is going to get you out of this one.'

William handed Kate the serrated steak knife, and with lightning speed, Kate grabbed Caitlin's left arm and ran the blade up it, digging deep.

William grabbed her head and pushed her under the water. He had kept the level low. Enough for her to drown but not so much that the floor would be swimming.

Caitlin kicked and made a fuss for a few moments.

'Quick, do the other arm,' Kate said.

William took the knife and ran it up Caitlin's right arm. He waited until the young woman had stopped struggling and then put the knife in her right hand, getting her prints on it. They watched as it slipped from her grasp.

'Let's get the hell out of here,' Kate said, and they took off their wet gloves and dried their hands. Kate took out a carrier bag and they put the gloves into it and slipped out of the apartment.

THIRTY-FIVE

Caitlin knew she didn't have long.

When she and her friends had talked about their personal safety when they were out and about, one thing they'd talked about was playing dead if they were being raped. Luckily, nobody had been through that ordeal to see if it worked, but that was the thought that sprang to mind when her two attackers were pushing her head underwater.

Her brief foray into karate lessons had got her up to yellow belt, but like many other things in Caitlin's life, it had become boring. That was the time to jump ship, when her interest waned. Just like her relationships.

She hadn't picked up much from the karate class – except a broken fingernail one time – but one thing she had remembered was, don't panic. Panic equals fear, which equals death.

If you can't fight, don't panic. Try to remember your surroundings, remember details about the person attacking you.

When Caitlin's head was pushed underwater, that was the time to try to hold her breath and ignore the pain that was zipping up her arms. She held her breath and went limp. She was either going to die or they would assume she was dead, and luckily for her, they thought she was either dead or had passed out from the loss of blood. Either way, they left.

She heard the front door being closed, then got out of the bath and grabbed two small towels to try to stop the bleeding. She roughly wrapped a towel round herself, then struggled through to the living room to grab her phone.

She got through to the operator, feeling her head spinning now. After telling them she had been attacked and her address, she staggered through to the hallway on shaky legs and managed to open the front door, before sliding down the wall and sitting in the hallway to wait for help.

THIRTY-SIX

'Are you sure?' Bracken said into his phone.

The control room operator assured him that this was indeed the case.

He hung up and looked at Kara. 'Caitlin Jordan just made a treble nine call. She was attacked in her apartment and left for dead. Her attackers are gone, but she's needing help.'

'Go then. Where does she live?'

'The flats on what used to be Greenbank Hospital.' He looked at the concrete tower before him and was about to make another comment about how places were being overrun with flats, but they didn't have time.

'Jimmy, with me,' Bracken said, and Kara held out her hand. Sullivan handed over the keys for his car.

Bracken and Sullivan walked outside, careful not

to go face first into either a snow bank or a puddle of mud.

Bracken once again used his Harry Potter skillset and weaved the car through the traffic without redesigning the front of the car on a corpie bus, shooting the car up Craiglockhart Avenue, across into Glenlockhart, right into The Steils and round to Greenbank.

Bracken and Sullivan made it into the flat just as the ambulance crew were getting Caitlin onto a stretcher.

'Is she okay?' Bracken asked, seeing her oxygen mask.

'We need to get her to the Royal as soon as,' one of the paramedics said. 'She's lost a lot of blood.'

'Caitlin, who did this?' Bracken asked.

Caitlin weakly pulled down the oxygen mask. 'Man and woman. Kara Page. Bracken.'

Then she was away. The detritus of her attack lay on the hallway floor. Uniforms were inside.

'Christ, using our names again,' Bracken said. He turned to a uniform. 'What was it like when you got here?' he asked.

'Pretty much as you see it now, sir,' the sergeant replied. 'Some of the towels I flung over there as I got fresh ones to try to stem the bleeding. She was in a bad way, but it looks like she's going to make it.'

'I wonder why they didn't make sure she was dead?' Sullivan said.

'She told me she played dead. They must have thought she was dead, then left.'

'Any of the neighbours see anything?'

'We haven't found anybody who saw anything. I have more bodies coming, so we can do a wider door-to-door. Forensics are on their way too.'

'Okay. Let us know if anything develops,' Bracken said. Then he called Kara and said they would meet her back at the station.

First, though, he wanted to go and talk to somebody.

THIRTY-SEVEN

'Mrs Bracken?' The young man was smiling as he approached Catherine. 'Sean sent me.'

It was a lie, but it got her attention.

'Who are you?' Catherine asked. She had been about to put the key in the lock of the bank's front door.

He was within five feet now. She could run if she wanted, albeit on a rather slippery pavement, or she could shout out for help, but she had been a copper's wife at one time and he knew that she would be level-headed.

'It doesn't matter who I am. But this is the point where you have to make a grown-up decision: you can either come with me right now or you can start shouting for help. One of those decisions will kill your daughter.'

He could see the fear land in her eyes, but he gave

her credit for not immediately shouting for some member of the public to help her, some innocent person who would get stabbed to death for interfering.

'Where's Sarah?' Catherine said, trying and failing to keep her voice from crumbling.

'I'm going to take you to her. That's the other choice you have: you come with me, get in my van, and we take a short drive to go and see her. But we're on the clock here; my friend is expecting me to call in exactly twelve minutes' time. Well, twelve minutes since I sent him a text telling him the clock had started and that was just before I spoke to you. The choice is yours; sit still, don't do anything stupid and I will text my friend. He has three phones. If you grab my phone and text the last number I sent a text to, he'll know it's not from me, and Sarah dies.'

'You've thought this all out, haven't you?' Catherine said.

'Yes, we have,' said Adam Malone.

Catherine got in the van.

THIRTY-EIGHT

'Who is it this time?' the old woman behind the reception glass asked. 'Wicked Witch of the West again?'

'I'm here to speak to Robert Marshall,' Bracken said.

'Have you booked an appointment?'

'Do we have to do this dance every time I come here?'

The woman had a look that suggested she had somehow trapped her pet hedgehog in her underwear that morning.

'I may be *dancing* in your eyes, Inspector, but I can assure you, I am doing the job that I get paid for every month. Now, I am sure that you would be quite happy dancing, but I prefer to keep this relationship on a business level.'

Bracken wondered what the hell she was talking about, and looked at Sullivan to see if he had any clue, but Sullivan just shrugged and mentally pushed the boss closer to the glass.

Bracken was just wondering if the woman was actually a patient here when Robert Marshall poked his head round the reception doorway. 'Buzz them in, please. I'm expecting them.'

The woman tutted and buzzed the door open.

'Dancing indeed,' Bracken heard the woman say. 'You wish.'

In the hallway through the door, Marshall was smiling as he stepped back from the lion's den.

'I know she's a crabby old boot, but she means well,' he said, leaning heavily on his walking stick.

'I heard that,' the woman said.

'Not you, Mrs McPherson. Another receptionist I know,' Marshall shouted back. 'I meant her,' he said in a whisper, as if Bracken hadn't got it the first time.

'I can still hear you.'

For a man with a walking stick, Marshall could shift when he wanted to. 'Bloody sciatica,' he said when they got to the lift. He looked past the detectives to the way they'd just come. 'Bloody woman's got ears like radar.' He kept his eyes on the office doorway to see if she'd heard that too, but they were out of striking distance.

'Some receptionists like to think they're doctors,' Sullivan said. 'Like the women in my doctor's practice. You would think they'd gone to medical school by the way they talk to you. One crow even asked me what my ailment was when I called up. Like I'd bloody well tell her over the phone.'

'They have wee blue tablets for that nowadays, Jimmy,' Bracken said, and Marshall chuckled as the lift door opened.

'Athlete's foot?' Sullivan said.

'Aye. That and a runny nose.' Bracken shook his head as the doors closed and they took the lift up to the second floor, where Marshall's office was.

They walked along and saw Fritz Meyer coming out of his own office. 'Ah, Chief Inspector. What a surprise. Back so soon?'

'Just investigating another matter, Doctor.'

'That's good then. Nothing wrong with Ailsa going on her trip?'

'No, nothing to do with that.'

'Good. Excellent. See you soon, I hope.'

Marshall unlocked his door and they walked in. 'Please, have a seat.'

They sat opposite him at his desk. This wasn't the business end of his profession; his patient room was on the floor below.

'What's so urgent, Sean?' Marshall asked.

'We found a connection between some of your patients.'

'Oh, yes? Which ones?'

'Meghan Fisher, Callum Darnley and Benedict Cuthbert.' Bracken left out Caitlin's name for the moment.

'Oh, yes, I remember them. What's the problem with them?'

'They're all dead. We think they were murdered, Robert, their deaths staged to look like suicides.'

'Good God. Who would want to murder them?'

'We were hoping you could tell us,' Sullivan said.

Marshall made a face like he was chewing the inside of his cheek in concentration. 'I know they all came to me for counselling,' he said at last. 'They had a drink problem, and the courts made them come here. They were all friends and unfortunately they'd been involved in the death of a young girl. Meghan crashed her car into another car and killed the little girl. The others were in the car with her.'

'And Callum Darnley was accused of bullying a girl at school and she hanged herself.'

'I can talk about the patients because they're dead, but I would still ask you to show respect for the parents.' Marshall held up a hand when he saw Bracken was about to speak. 'I know Darnley is dead. But Peter Fisher isn't.'

'I understand, Robert. But we still need to look into this.'

Marshall nodded, having got his point across. 'They were at school together. Thick as thieves they were. This was from Meghan herself. They would meet up and go drinking, and of course spoilt little sods that they were, their rich parents always covered for them. You can imagine how that went when Meghan had the crash. She was the only one who walked away without a scratch. Callum and Benedict were hurt, Benedict the most. Which made him even more irresponsible. Meghan told them that they were all invincible. Some of the other kids they hung out with believed it too. That's why one of them walked along the edge of a roof one night after they'd been binge drinking. Benedict told him that nothing could happen to him. But the young man fell to his death. It was ruled misadventure.'

'We believe the parents of the kids who died came to family therapy.'

'Yes. I remember it well. Ailsa took those sessions. You know how she killed those people who dodged justice? I think she would have killed those rich kids at the time if she'd had a mind to.'

'Listen, Robert, I'm telling you this in confidence, because I need your help. We think that maybe some of the parents are getting revenge for their kids. William

Watkins, Kate Lamb. Maybe the parents of the boy who fell off the roof. We found Benedict Cuthbert dead this morning.'

'The boy who fell ten years ago was called Frederick Young. Both of his parents are dead. I heard about them dying. The mother died of cancer, the father died an alcoholic. This was years ago.'

Bracken looked at Sullivan before looking back at Marshall. 'Maybe it's just two suspects we're looking for, Watkins and the Lamb woman.'

'Do you think they could have joined forces, Dr Marshall?' Sullivan asked.

'It's possible. Sometimes a group therapy session will be held so that grieving parents can help each other.'

'Thanks, Robert,' Bracken said. He stood up, followed by Sullivan.

Marshall stood up from behind his desk. 'Any time. You know, I'm looking forward to the little excursion. I wish it was on Sunday, so Ailsa could be with parishioners, but she's only too happy to be talking with a minister. The Sunday service will come soon after her release. I have to admit, I'll be quite happy moving to the country to live. Having to drive up a little hill to get to our house. Somewhere that no ordinary car can easily get to. No offence, Sean.'

'None taken. I'll hire a Range Rover when I come to see you.'

'That's the spirit. I'm already prepared.'

'Kara Page and I are looking forward to going with you both. See you then.'

They walked out of the office and saw Fritz Meyer coming back along to his. Bracken turned to Sullivan and issued him with a couple of orders before turning back again.

Meyer smiled at Bracken. 'You're here that often, you'll be getting invited to the office Christmas party.'

'Trust me, next December I'll be there. But listen, could I have a chat with Ailsa for five minutes?'

'Why of course, Sean. Come along and we'll get you upstairs.'

Bracken nodded to Sullivan. 'See you downstairs.'

Bracken and Meyer rode the lift up one floor, then they went through the security checkpoints.

'I'll leave you both alone. With the orderly outside, of course,' Meyer said, smiling. 'See you soon, Sean.'

'My my, twice in one week,' Ailsa Connolly said. 'To what do I owe the honour?'

'It would have been twice in one week when we went on your trip,' Bracken reminded her.

'Ah, but this is a little extra visit. Two I was expecting; this one in the middle I was not. Therefore, there's something you need from me. Please have a seat.'

Bracken waited until she'd sat in the low-down chair, the struggling-to-get-up-and-kill-you seat, before sitting down on his over-stuffed, stiff chair. The one that gave an unsuspecting victim half a chance if things went sour very quickly. Some people might scrabble to find a fireside poker, but luckily Bracken's hand-to-hand skills were sharp.

'I don't have much time, so I'll get straight to the point: William Watkins and Kate Lamb.'

'Olympic figure-skating champions?'

Bracken knew she was just fucking with him. He had to let her think she had control of the situation.

'You know who they are, Ailsa.'

'Do I? Or am I just prolonging the conversation because there's so little of it in here?'

'Fine, Ailsa. I don't have time for these games.' He started to get up, but she smiled and waved him back down.

'These people are important to you, I can see that. So they're involved with a case you're working on. From the news, I see that Meghan Fisher, Callum Darnley and his father were murdered. You think that my two previous patients are involved. Who else is dead?'

Bracken hesitated for a brief second, and it was all that Ailsa needed. 'The body of a man found on a building site this morning? Benedict Cuthbert.'

'How did you know? We haven't released a name yet.'

'Benedict was one of the dirty four. Caitlin Jordan was the last name. Somebody better get hold of her. Her life could be in danger too.'

'She was attacked earlier.'

'Ah. Now you think that there are two parents out there exacting revenge.'

'It's a theory we're working on.'

She sat with her fingers steepled for a moment, thinking. 'Tell me how Benedict died. Not just how the news is reporting it.'

'Looks like he was hit with a hammer in the head and he had a kneecap smashed before he was thrown off the top of the new construction.'

'Tell me the details of the other deaths.'

He did. Meghan with the pills and the vodka. Callum hanging himself. Caitlin slashing her arms in a bath of hot water but surviving.

'All made to look like suicides. Interesting. Ultimately, they knew you would find out, so this was just a time-buying exercise. A suicide wouldn't be investigated as passionately as a murder. Strange how they targeted all four when only two of them were to blame for another's death – Meghan for drunk-driving and Callum for the bullying that made a girl take her own life. The other two were in the car when Meghan crashed but were really bystanders. Why kill them too?'

'Maybe just because they were there, and the killers are dealing with them all. Possibly to draw the attention away from the two families who have dead children. To draw our attention away from Watkins and Lamb.'

'Could be, Sean, but you know as well as I do that killing two more people is far more risky.' She put her fingers down. 'You know that, so you're here to see if I can reveal anything more just from the therapy sessions I had with them. Unfortunately, I can't reveal any details.'

Bracken blew out a breath and stood up. 'It was worth a try.'

'However, if I were a detective, I would look into the backgrounds of the family members,' Ailsa said.

'We did. Although Basil Darnley looks like the slimiest of them all, there was nothing there.'

'Nothing concrete. Think about it, Sean. Now, how is that lovely daughter of yours?'

'She's fine.'

'No, she isn't. That's why you're fidgety today. You're tense. I've only seen that in you when you're worried about Sarah.'

'If a child uses text shortcuts, then suddenly doesn't, what would that tell you?'

'Go look for her, Sean. She's in trouble. That's what I would say.'

'See you later,' he said. Then, when he was outside her wing, he ran.

THIRTY-NINE

They were in the warmth of the incident room, Bracken once again at the helm.

'We talked to Ailsa Connolly, but she wouldn't give us anything helpful enough to get an insight into William Watkins and Kate Lamb. Confidentiality and all that. But the couple are in the wind just now. Their driving licences were never updated from their old addresses. DS Gale and DC Lennox checked out their last-known addresses, but the houses are empty.'

Just then there was a knock on the incident room door and a uniformed sergeant poked his head in. 'Sorry to interrupt, but there's a man here to speak with DCI Bracken. Said he'll only speak with you and DI Sullivan, sir.'

Bracken looked puzzled but left the room with Sullivan and they followed the sergeant along to an interview room. The sergeant opened the door and led them inside.

A tall, blond-haired man stood up from the table. 'I'm Glen King. I'm the man who was having an affair with Meghan Fisher.'

Bracken nodded to the sergeant. 'Thanks. We'll take it from here.'

As the door closed, Bracken indicated for the man to take a seat and they sat opposite him.

'I know this looks bad, but when I read in the paper that you're looking for a tall man who was last seen at the nightclub with Meghan, I knew I couldn't stand back any longer, no matter what happens. You see, I didn't kill Meghan. We were planning on running away together.'

'She left a note saying that she was having an affair, but nobody believed it.'

'We were very careful. We had arranged to meet at the nightclub last Saturday. Her fiancé is very nice and not suspicious, but we couldn't risk being seen together, and since he would be in Dublin, we figured he couldn't just walk in on her.'

'We saw you leave the club with her on the security camera footage,' Sullivan said. 'Not leave the building but hover near the entrance to the offices.'

'We just left the nightclub to talk. You need to learn semaphore just to talk to each other in those places. So we stepped out into the corridor to talk. She was well drunk, though. Much drunker than I'd expected her to be, and to be honest, I was hoping she wasn't getting cold feet. She assured me she wasn't and that she was just playing the part of the bride-to-be.'

'What was your end game with her?' Bracken asked.

'She was going to split up with Rodney before the wedding. I mean, I don't think he has the balls to kill her, and he was in Dublin. Anyway, she was bored with him, and Meghan and I had fun together.'

'Her friends were with her on Saturday,' Sullivan said. 'Weren't you worried that one of them would see you?'

'Friends? That's a laugh. Hangers-on more like. None of them care. Besides, we were watching them getting off with men in the club and half of them are married. It didn't concern us.'

'You were the last one seen with her so far as we can establish,' Bracken said. 'It's not looking good for you.'

'Look, would I come in here and tell you this if I murdered her?'

'Somebody with balls might,' Bracken answered.

'I didn't kill her. I loved her. Despite her flaws.'

'We'll need a statement. Fingerprints. DNA,' Bracken said.

'Anything you need. I'll take a lie detector test, anything you need to help catch her killer.' King brought out his driving licence and showed them. Bracken took a photo of it.

'Where were you on Monday night? Tuesday morning? Last night?'

'I had a business meeting down in London with some of my colleagues. I'm an architect. We flew down on Monday morning, first thing, and flew back up this morning. We were talking to financial advisors about a new project, trying to get funding.'

'You're an architect?' Sullivan said.

'Yes. It's how I met Meghan. I knew Peter Fisher before I knew her. He's a wizard with financial things.'

'You got on well with her father, sounds like,' Bracken said.

'He's her stepfather. And yes, we got on well. She told me she was only marrying Rodney because he was from a wealthy family.'

'We'll need to see some proof of your flights.'

King pulled out papers from his inside pocket; flight ticket stubs, a hotel booking receipt. 'Call them. Call my employer.' He put the papers on the desk and wrote out a telephone number. 'That's their number there.'

'We'll check it out. Leave us a contact number.'

Again, King wrote a number down on the piece of

paper. 'I hope you catch this bastard soon. He ruined my chance at happiness with Meghan.'

They let him out of the room, and went back to the incident room and explained to the others.

'What if we just let our murderer walk out the door?' Doc said.

'He had proof of being down in London. He's not our killer. He gave us a statement and DNA. He's not our man though.'

They were heading to their desks to work on their computers when Bracken's phone rang. He talked, then hung up and walked over to Kara's office.

'Ma'am, I have something I need to deal with.'

'Is it something to do with this case?'

'No. It's something to do with an old case.'

'Is it something you can talk about?'

He looked at his watch.

'Give me the edited version,' she said.

'It's about a bank robbery.'

FORTY

Ten years ago

The adrenaline was coming fast for DI Sean Bracken, as it would be for his colleagues too, he imagined. DCI Billy Burton stood at the front of the room, the scaled drawing on the whiteboard behind him. They were going over it again, and if anybody wasn't sure, they would go over it once more.

Nobody said they didn't understand.

'As the PF said, this isn't an ideal situation, but if we collar them outside, then we don't have much proof that an actual bank robbery was going to take place. The most we could get them on is intent to rob, but that wouldn't guarantee a conviction, as you all know.

Firearms charges certainly, but again it's touch and go. That's why we've gone this route. It's the lesser of two evils. Any questions?'

'You buying in the pub afterwards?' DI Bob Long shouted, and they all laughed.

'Never let it be said I don't put my hand in my pocket. If we all get back here tonight in one piece, then I might stretch to buying a half for everybody. Just one, mind. The rest of you can bugger off.'

They all laughed as they stood up. Burton waved Bracken over.

'Watch the new guy, Sean. Robertson is a good guy, but this is his first outing. Keep an eye on him.'

'He'll be fine.' Famous last words, Bracken would think later on.

'Good lad. Let's go beat the clock.'

It was March, not quite ice cream weather and only the foolish would attempt a walk along the promenade without a heavy jacket and a backup plan.

Round the back of Leith police station, the men were getting into their cars. Six men, three cars, all of them waiting for the phone call. Bracken answered when it came.

'*The last customer just left,*' the shaky voice said.

'You remember what we planned. Get going now. Everybody out of sight. We'll be there in two minutes.'

Bracken hung up and flashed his headlights. The other two cars followed behind as he drove round to Mitchell Street and down Constitution Street, across Baltic Street. The entrance to the bank's car park was through a gate on the left.

This was one of the points where it could go haywire. What if they were watching?

It was a risk the police were willing to take. The feeling was, the robbers wouldn't be sitting too close to the bank. They would follow the armoured truck in and wait until the cash was taken inside. Then they would load it, bit by bit, into their own van. No confrontation was to occur outside of the building.

Two-man team, both of them moving the bags to the van. It had to be a small van, as the turning into the car park was too tight for one of the bigger trucks.

Bracken pulled in and parked close to the wall nearest to Constitution Street, and he got out with the new guy, Rab Robertson.

'You nervous?' he asked Robertson as they walked casually across the car park to the back entrance.

'No, I'm fine,' the younger detective answered.

Then they were in through the door, which had been left unlocked for them. There were no visible locks on the outside of the door, so there were no locks to pick. The only way the doors opened was when somebody from inside opened them. This was also a car park for customers, but they had to walk round to the front of the building to get in.

The door swung in easily and the bank was eerily quiet.

Through in the main banking hall, the double doors to the outside had been closed and locked. The tellers were all downstairs in the basement and this was where two of the detectives got to play teller for a few minutes. And have a shooter pointed at them.

'Just stay calm, son, and everything will be fine. None of these jokers want to end up dead, and the plan is, when they see they're outgunned, they'll drop their weapons.'

'It shouldn't take that long,' Robertson said, not anticipating a hostage situation. There wouldn't be one, Bracken knew for a fact.

Once the other four men, including Bob Long, were inside, the back door was locked again. It had to be business as usual in case the robbers were watching the guards. The guards couldn't be seen to just walk in or else the robbers would know something was off.

'We'll be through the back in the offices,' Bracken said to the others, indicating himself and Robertson. 'You two will be behind the counter, pretending to do bank stuff, and you two will be round the corner at the other end. The van should be here any minute, so get crack-a-lacking.' A phrase he would never use again.

Bob Long went behind the counter with a sergeant and the other two went to their positions. A couple of minutes later, there was a knock on the back door.

The guards were let in. Each of them was wearing a crash helmet and carrying canvas bags of money.

Three trips they made, and it was during the last one that it kicked off. Two men in balaclavas pushed the guards inside, one of them pointing a sawn-off. This was Frank Malone.

The two detectives held up their hands, playing the part of scared tellers to perfection.

'Right, you two pair of bastards,' Billy Turner said, 'grab a bag each and get it back out to our van. Do something stupid and you don't get to go home tonight.'

Both detectives picked up a pair of bags each from behind the counter. Bracken and Robertson moved out of the back office, each of them pointing their gun.

'Police, drop the fucking guns!' Robertson shouted.

Bracken didn't know if it was panic or instinct, but Billy Turner turned round and aimed his gun at Bracken. By then, though, Bracken had fired, and the bullet caught Turner in the chest.

Frank Malone had dropped his shotgun amongst all the screaming that they were police and they would shoot if he didn't drop the weapon. He lay down on the floor with his arms outstretched.

Bracken ran to Turner and tried to stem the flow of blood while somebody called for a medic.

Billy Turner was already gone by the time Malone was taken out and the ambulance crew got in.

FORTY-ONE

'Robertson panicked or was overeager, one of the two, but Bob and his partner hadn't got their guns ready yet. Robertson shouted the warning just a split second too early. He never worked firearms again. I was investigated but was cleared of any wrongdoing. And now their sons want revenge on me.'

'I'm not letting you go alone,' Kara said.

'It's just a hunch; I'm not a hundred per cent certain. But if my little girl is in trouble, then I'm going to do whatever it takes to help her.'

'I can get the firearms team deployed in minutes. They can be there, backing you up.'

'They might kill her. They want me, but they might get spooked and do something stupid.'

'Jesus, Sean. If this was any other member of my team, I would be in an awkward position, but this is the man who saved my life I'm talking to. You didn't hesitate when the time came, and I sure as hell am not going to sit back and let them ambush you and then walk away.'

'They're dangerous people. Adam Malone and Mark Turner, sons of two bank robbers. One who died on the job, the other who died of a heart attack in prison two years later. And to think I met Adam Malone on Saturday night. The bastard must have been scoping me out.'

'Do what you have to do, Sean, but there's no way I'm letting you walk in there alone.'

'He said they have Catherine as well. That's two of them. I want them to take me in return for their release. I have half an hour and then they'll kill them. He let me hear them talk, so I know they're alive, but for how long, I don't know.'

'How many of the team are firearms trained?'

'Two that I know of.'

'Right, here's what we're going to do. I can have it set up in five minutes. And no arguing with me, DCI Bracken.'

The car park had a few cars in it but none for the old bank building. Pulling his car into it brought back memories. After the shooting, Bracken had left the firearms unit and returned to normal detective duties. So had Bob Long. Rab Robertson had gone back to uniform, and the last Bracken had heard, the man was a DI down in the Borders. Hopefully without a firearm.

There was an old van parked by the back door of the bank, and Bracken knew the door to the building would be ajar. He wouldn't be able to get in otherwise.

He got out of the car and walked over to the door, expecting it to come firing open at any second, but nobody was there, waiting to greet him. He pulled it open and stepped in from the cold, although the temperature wasn't much warmer than outside.

He walked through to the banking hall, past the corridor he and Robertson had come charging out of, and walked towards where the counters had once been.

The click of the gun wasn't exactly in his ear but it wasn't on the moon either.

'Tick-tock, Sean. You're late. I told you what would happen if you were late.'

Bracken looked round to see Mark Turner pointing a Glock handgun at him.

'You have me now, Mark. Let Sarah and Catherine go.'

'Did I tell you I was going to do that?'

'I assumed you were.'

Turner laughed. 'You know what assume means.'

'They're safe for now, Sean,' Adam Malone said, stepping into the hall from the other side of where the counters used to be.

His words were cut off by the front door being unlocked and a man and woman stepping inside.

'What the hell?' Turner said. Then he looked at Bracken. 'If you move, I'll kill you all.'

They saw the woman was holding out a portfolio, just like the one the other agent had shown Turner. He knew it contained photos and sheets of paper with details of the building on it.

The man was older than she was, and overweight.

'This is the main hall,' the woman said, then stopped. 'Oh, I'm sorry. I didn't realise there were any more clients in here.'

'I've already leased the place,' Turner said as the woman walked closer. He held the gun behind his back.

Malone tucked his gun into the back of his jeans and walked over to them.

'I'm sorry. There's been a mistake,' he said to the woman. 'You'll have to leave.'

'Now, that's where you're wrong, squire,' Tam Gale said, and he saw Malone's hand go behind his back. He put an arm in front of Izzie, took a step forward and headbutted Malone in the face.

Malone fell backwards, his gun skidding across the floor. As he hit the deck, he rolled and reached for the gun, a few feet away.

Gale stepped forward and pointed his Glock at the man's face. 'Your finger touches it, I'll take your face off.'

At the same time that Gale had put an arm in front of Izzie, Turner had started to lift his gun, but he felt cold steel touch his head below the ear.

Then the firearms teams stormed in from the back and through the front door, dressed in black, holding rifles, shouting and screaming.

Sullivan holstered his Glock.

'I need to find Sarah and Catherine, Jimmy,' said Bracken.

'Lads, this way,' Sullivan said, but the team commander led the way. They split up into teams and Bracken pointed at a doorway.

'That leads to the vaults. Malone came from there.'

They made their way down the stairs and cleared each room, until they found Sarah and Catherine. They were tied to chairs and gagged.

Sarah started crying and shouting when she saw her dad.

'I thought he was going to kill us,' she said once her gag was removed. 'You were right.'

Catherine was shaken but smiled when the gag was taken off her. 'I hate to admit it, but Sarah's right: you were right.'

'Police Scotland at your service, ma'am.' Bracken turned to Sullivan. 'Good work there, Jimmy. God knows how you moved so quietly.'

'Tam did a good job too. How did you know he's firearms trained?'

'I read through his record before he and Doc came on board. If he was complete mince, he wouldn't have been with us. He has a bit of a reputation of course, but I'm sure we'll iron that out of him.'

William and Kate opened the door that led into the garage. They didn't put the light on; they didn't have to: the shaft of light from the house was enough to illuminate the two guests who were sitting on the floor, hands tied, and tied to each other.

The real William and Kate.

'Sorry about the discomfort, but I have to admit, it was fun playing...well, William and Kate. We thought of ourselves as you both, and it was very kind of you to lend us your names for a little while.'

'Yes, it was fun,' Kate said to the real Kate Lamb.

'However, let us make it up to you.' William held up two bottles of vodka, waving them in front of Real William. 'Let's have a little drink.'

Kate moved forward to Real Kate and pulled her gag down. 'Let's have a drink.'

The sleeping tablets had already been crushed and put into the vodka bottles.

'Congratulations, Dad,' Sarah said, packing the last of her things into a box.

'On what?' he said, hoping that he wasn't pulling a beamer.

'You know.' She looked at Catherine. 'Tell him, Mum.'

'On you and Chaz finally admitting that you're now boyfriend and girlfriend.'

'Jesus. Could you two be more embarrassing?'

'Look, dear, everybody else could see that you were dating. You were the only one who couldn't see it. I knew Chaz could, but she was waiting for you to come round from the dark side.'

'Why do I feel like I'm a fifteen year old who's just been handed his first rubber johnny?'

'Dad, please. I know I'm an adult, but I don't want to hear my parents talk about such stuff.'

'You brought it up.'

'Anyway, we can all have a wee drink in the pub one night, if you promise to leave your manky old johnny at home.'

'This conversation has gone downhill and I'm leaving. Just one more box to go in my car and that's your lot.' He looked round at the furniture. 'You sure none of this is yours?'

'I'm sure. It was all here when I moved in. All my stuff is boxed.'

They went down to their cars and Bracken put the box in. He had solved one problem but still had the main one to solve.

Where were William Watkins and Kate Lamb?

They drove away from Marchmont and headed down to Leith. To The Shore, where Catherine had a flat. Sarah would be staying back home for the foreseeable future.

The apartments were fairly new, one block of them overlooking the Water of Leith. Bracken knew they would be comfortable here. Mark Turner and Adam Malone were going away for a long time.

'You staying for a drink?' Catherine asked once they'd unloaded the boxes into her flat.

Bracken was looking out into the darkness, at the lights from the flats on the other side reflecting on the cold water. At the snow around the edge of the river. He thought about Robert and Ailsa and their plans to live in a croft miles from anywhere. He turned to face her.

'No, thanks. I'll get off home.'

'You need to get yourself a place soon, Sean. Set down some roots again.'

'I will.' The thought was nagging at him. Then something hit him. 'I have to go.'

He kissed his daughter goodbye, let himself out and took the lift down. Back in his car, he floored it as much as you could floor a car on an icy road next to a river without first donning a wetsuit.

He drove up Leith Walk and cut over west until he was driving up Bruntsfield, heading for Morningside.

He reached Robert Marshall's house and was glad to see there was a light on in the living room and that the old boy hadn't left his front door open again.

Bracken stopped in the street, wondering if he was doing the right thing. But it was only one little question. No big deal.

He stepped out into the bitter cold and saw Marshall's little VW Beetle sitting in the drive. He walked over to it. The car was sitting in front of the attached garage. There were footprints all around it and he could see the car had been moved recently, its tyre tracks clear in the snow on the drive.

The garage door should have been replaced years ago, but Marshall had said it would ruin the integrity of the whole house if he got some modern door.

Bracken walked up to the front door and rang the bell. Marshall answered with a smile.

'Come on in, Sean,' he said, leaning on his walking stick.

Bracken stepped into the warmth but stopped short.

'I was coming round to see if you were prepared for tomorrow's little trip with Ailsa,' Bracken said.

'Everything's ready to go, Sean. Are you ready?'

An overnight stay out in the wilds of Scotland wasn't exactly appealing at this time of year, but at least they'd be staying in a hotel.

'You told me you were ready for you and Ailsa to finally be free of the city and live in the country, but I was thinking that your old Beetle isn't exactly the car for that job.'

'That's why I have the Land Rover!' Marshall beamed a smile at Bracken.

'When did you get a Land Rover, Robert?'

'I bought it from one of the orderlies. He had bought it from the poor nurse who was murdered. He said it creeped him out. He hadn't registered it yet, so I jumped at the chance. It runs great.'

'Where is it?'

'In my garage. I just moved it here. It was parked in the hospital, tucked away in a little corner, but the management said it had to move because it wasn't registered. You want a look at it?'

Bracken thought back to when Kara Page's house

had been set on fire. A small dark-green Land Rover with a short wheelbase had been seen coming out of the lane behind her house and taking off at high speed.

'I'd like that, if you don't mind.'

'Absolutely. The door's open.'

'Didn't we just have a conversation about you leaving your front door open, Robert?'

'Ah! That was about me leaving the front door open. This is the garage door.'

Marshall pulled on a thick coat and they went back out into the cold. He pulled the door shut. 'Yes, it's locked,' he said.

They walked over to the garage door and Marshall opened it. Inside was the green Land Rover.

With two people sitting in the front seats.

Very much dead.

FORTY-THREE

Blue light bounced off the snow, the houses and everywhere else it could think of.

Kara Page had driven up in her BMW from the guest house.

'Ed and Bob wanted to come along for the ride,' she told Bracken.

'Did they start greetin' like wee boys when you said no?'

'They just went in a huff. But they're boys who are old enough to drown their sorrows with a few stiff whiskies, so no harm done.'

'It seems the only way I get to see you is to turn up at a crime scene,' Chaz said to Bracken, smiling.

'Be careful what you wish for,' Kara said. 'I only stay under the same roof as him and already he's driving me daft.'

'What nonsense is this now? You been listening to my dad again? If you're not careful, he'll change everything you knew about history. Don't get him started on the moon landings. He thinks because the images sent back were remarkable and CCTV footage from petrol stations looks like it's been filmed on a toaster, then it was all a hoax.'

'What do you believe, Sean?'

'I believe the moon is made from cheese.'

They went inside and Bracken felt sorry for Marshall. The man was sitting on his settee with a blanket around his shoulders, shivering, not from the cold but from finding two corpses in his car.

'I know you've told DCI Bracken about this, Dr Marshall, but I need you to go over it with me again,' Kara said.

Marshall looked at her. 'I don't know anything about those two in the car. I don't know how they got there.'

'They both have vomit coming out of their mouths, suggesting poisoning or something along those lines. And you do know them; they're the people we've been looking for. William Watkins and Kate Lamb. You know them, don't you?'

He made eye contact with her. 'I do. They were patients of mine in group therapy. Ask Sean. He knows I know them. I haven't made it a secret.'

'This is where we have a problem, Doctor. You knew the other victims. You knew what they were like. Spoilt rich kids.'

'Doesn't mean to say I'd kill anybody. As you can see, I'm disabled. I'm hardly in a position to kill anybody. Anyway, shouldn't you be interviewing me down at the station?' Marshall said.

'We will, don't worry. Stand up.'

Marshall stood up, leaning on his walking stick, the blanket slipping off.

Kara turned towards Bracken, who stepped forward. 'Robert Marshall, I'm arresting you on suspicion of murder.'

'I can't believe this. I didn't do anything.'

A uniform stepped forward with handcuffs, but Bracken shook his head and the man stepped back.

'Take him to the West End,' he said and watched as Marshall was led out.

'I'll go to the station now. You do what you've got to do,' Kara said.

Marshall stopped at the front door, turned and made eye contact with Bracken.

Then he was gone.

FORTY-FOUR

Bracken was glad to see the old dragon wasn't behind the reception desk when he got there. Kara had made a phone call and Fritz Meyer was waiting for him.

'I just stay round at the Braids,' he said. 'It sounded urgent on the phone. Is everything okay?'

'I'd like to talk with you and Ailsa. I'll explain when we get up there; save me explaining twice. You're going to need to be there for her, Doctor.'

'Oh my. This does sound serious.'

'More than you know.'

They took the lift up to the secure wing, and the night-shift orderlies let them pass through the security doors without a problem.

Ailsa Connolly had been forewarned of their impending arrival and was already seated in her chair.

'Has something happened to Robert?' she asked immediately.

Bracken pointed to the chair opposite Ailsa while he sat on the couch. Meyer sat down.

'I have some bad news about Robert, I'm afraid,' Bracken said.

Ailsa's mouth fell open, but he held up a hand.

'He's been arrested for murder.'

'What?' Ailsa's face turned pale and she looked shocked.

'You're kidding,' Meyer said, his brow furrowing. 'I don't understand. Who has he murdered?'

'Allegedly. Two of his former patients. Maybe more. I can't go into too much detail, as he's only just been taken in for questioning, but it's not looking good.'

'Oh my God. I don't believe it,' Ailsa said and she sat back in the chair. 'My husband, a killer.'

Bracken looked at her, the irony not lost on him. 'Your first day release under supervision is tomorrow. Kara Page, Robert and I were going to accompany you. Obviously, that won't happen now.'

He could see the disappointment on her face.

'I have an idea, Chief Inspector,' Meyer said. 'Why don't I take Robert's place?'

Bracken looked at him, then looked at Ailsa. 'How do you feel about that? Would you still want to go ahead, even though your husband can't make it?'

'I think it would be wise, Ailsa,' Meyer said. 'You've come this far.'

'What's the point in it all now?' Ailsa shook her head. 'I don't even feel like it.'

'Listen, if it turns out that Robert did kill those people, that doesn't mean you shouldn't be allowed to carry on with your life. You've made good headway this far. Don't throw it all away now. I'll come along with Sean and Kara to give you support. It will be fine, Ailsa.'

'You really think I should go?' She looked at both men in turn.

'I think you should,' Bracken answered.

Ailsa thought about it some more. 'Okay, but you both have to promise me you'll be there. I can't do this alone. I need your support. Dr Meyer?'

Meyer smiled. 'I'll be there. I've always been here for you, Ailsa. I'm not about to fail you now.'

'Okay. I'll go.'

'Oh come, Dr Marshall,' Jimmy Sullivan said. 'William Watkins and Kate Lamb were patients of yours, weren't they?'

Next to him, Izzie sat stone-faced.

'Yes, they were my patients when they were in group therapy.'

'What about the others? The kids who were murdered?'

'You know they were. I counselled them for alcohol abuse.'

Izzie sat forward. 'You admit to having listened to the problems of the spoilt rich kids. Did that make you angry, Robert? When you saw them getting away with it? Did it make you want to punish them? To teach them a lesson they would never forget? A permanent lesson?'

'No.'

Sullivan tapped the table between them. 'Let's talk about the Land Rover.'

'Let's not.'

Sullivan smiled. 'Oh dear, a psychologist trying to use psychology against the poor, dumb detectives.' He shook his head. 'Let's talk about the Land Rover. You see, this was one thing that got away from us. It was seen booting away from the small lane behind Detective Superintendent Page's house. Whoever was driving it must have set fire to the house, leaving DSup Page inside, waiting to die.'

'Not necessarily,' Marshall answered. 'What if... the person driving the Land Rover was merely there to help, saw the house on fire, then barely escaped with his or her life, and panicked, fleeing from the scene. It's a theory that any good QC could come up with.'

Sullivan gave a little chuckle. 'Good one. Good luck getting a jury to go with that. You see, they'll be a jury made up of the general public. Maybe not a jury of your peers, maybe not everyone will be a psychologist or a doctor, but don't expect them to be dumb. Somebody driving away from the house while there just happens to be a killer inside doing the business? Any decent jury member would scoff at such nonsense.'

'You bought the Land Rover from a member of staff, didn't you?' Izzie said.

Marshall gave out a deep breath, signalling he was bored now. 'Yes.'

'Who is this member of staff?'

'It was an orderly. He would talk about cars non-stop. He was friends with Maxine Campbell, the nurse who's no longer with us, God rest her soul. He was going to do it up but didn't have the time. I mentioned that I would be retiring soon and going to live in the country. He said he was going to sell the Land Rover and asked whether I'd be interested. I said yes. You know the rest. I parked it in my garage, and tonight somebody put two dead people in it. Or two people who were dying. Only the pathologist will be able to give you the answers on that.'

'You see, I think that you suspected who the two killers were. It pissed you off so much that they were the ones killing those youngsters that you decided to take the matter into your own hands. Kill them. Punish them for what they did. Isn't that the truth, Dr Marshall?'

'Do I look like somebody who's physically capable of killing two people and putting them in the front of my car?'

'You've talked to a lot of nasty people in your time,

Doctor,' Izzie said. 'You know what resolve some people have when they put their minds to it.'

'I'm not physically able to deal with killing people.'

'If it wasn't you who killed them, then who was it?' Sullivan asked.

'I have no idea.'

'You have no idea because it was you. Let's face it, that walking stick is there for show, isn't it?'

'Don't be ridiculous.'

'Ridiculous, is it? Yet every year we hear about benefits cheats who go about their everyday life with a walking stick, just like the one you have, and are then filmed going to the gym, or sky diving, or white-water rafting. You get my point.'

'Yes, I see what you're driving at. You think I'm faking this, and under the cover of darkness I turn into Vigilante Man.'

'That's it exactly. Mr Vigilante Man. Or should I say, *Doctor* Vigilante Man?'

'You have no idea what you're talking about.'

'I know a lot more than you think I do. I know that you're going to be taken to the cells, and you won't face a judge until Monday morning. How your weekend goes is up to you.'

'I have nothing more to say.'

FORTY-SIX

Bracken was tired but not half as tired-looking as Kara was.

'You didn't sleep well last night, I take it?' he asked her.

'I think I got two hours, if I was lucky.'

Bracken sat up a little straighter and hoped the airbags in the BMW wouldn't explode willy-nilly and would do the job should they be called into action.

He was relieved when Kara pulled her car into the back car park of the new Royal Edinburgh wing, where Ailsa Connolly would be waiting for them.

'We're going in a minibus with blacked-out windows,' he said, 'so you'll be able to get your head down for a little while and nobody will be able to see you. We'll be the only ones who hear you snoring.'

'Women don't snore, Sean. We just breathe a little heavily.'

'Do you dream of unicorns at night?' he asked with a grin.

'You don't want to know what I dream about.'

No more snow had fallen, and the forecast was for cold but clear skies. In Bracken's mind, clear skies didn't necessarily mean good weather.

Upstairs, Ailsa was dressed in a white shirt and black trousers. Meyer was dressed like he was going on an Arctic expedition, with a heavy winter coat on. He was holding a woollen hat with a pompom on top, something that looked like he had knitted it himself.

'Are we ready for the off then?' Meyer asked.

'How's Robert doing?' Ailsa asked.

'He was booked in last night and he'll spend the weekend in the cells before being taken in front of a judge on Monday morning.'

'Did he ask for a lawyer?'

'Not yet. One will be appointed on Monday if he doesn't procure one himself.'

Ailsa looked at the floor before looking back at Bracken, and this time there were tears in her eyes. 'Why would he do that?'

'He felt he was getting revenge for the young people who were murdered. When he found out that they were murdered in the same way as two of their victims, he wanted revenge, plain and simple. He knew how to get in touch with William Watkins and Kate Lamb, and he lured them to their deaths. I think he was going to dispose of them later.'

'I still can't believe it.' She turned away and put on a winter jacket. She wasn't wearing any makeup, but she was a beautiful woman without it.

They made their way downstairs to the van, and Bracken wondered what would happen if Ailsa tried to make a run for it. Would she be able to outrun him? With his fitness level, a small child would be able to outrun him.

Ailsa didn't attempt to outrun anybody but got into the minibus without any fuss.

Kara sat in the back with her, and despite there being enough room to transport a five-a-side football team and all their gear, Fritz Meyer wanted to sit up front in the passenger seat.

Oh, God, Bracken thought. *Don't tell me he's expecting conversation.* He'd always met Meyer on a professional level, and this was like going camping with your school and trying to make conversation with your teacher.

What would have been maybe an hour's drive in summer took longer because the roads were a little bit slick in places, and very slick once they hit the country road west of Falkirk.

'God's own country,' Meyer said.

Bracken thought the man had dozed off for a while, but he was looking out of the window like a tourist in Texas, where everything would no doubt look miniature. The Falkirk Wheel would appear as a bathtub toy in downtown Dallas.

Bracken had to admit that this was indeed God's own country. Covered in snow just now, the hills would draw more visitors in the summer, but right now it was cold.

Another half hour along the A891 with Glasgow to their south and they were approaching their destination, a small village called Killearn in the Stirling council area. The very epitome of *fuck all to do*. There was a small cemetery on the outskirts of town, which was probably as close to a funfair as the locals were going to get.

At the first mini-roundabout, a sign welcomed them to Killearn. Main Street was quite long and it had a supermarket, Bracken saw. And an original red phone box. Further up, the road swept round to the right and they saw the large church come into view.

Bracken slowed down as they drove past and turned into the village hall car park. He followed the road round to the church car park, where two cars were parked, and stopped next to them.

'You ready, Ailsa?' he asked her.

'As ready as I'll ever be.'

He turned off the engine and they got out into air that felt sharper and colder than the air they'd just left.

FORTY-SEVEN

'Welcome!' the church's minister said, greeting them with a smile. 'I'm David Cruikshank. We haven't met, but we've spoken on the phone several times. Come on through to the Sunday school classroom and I'll make some tea.'

'Thank you for letting me come here today,' Ailsa said.

'God welcomes all his children.'

Meyer took his pompom hat off and Bracken was glad he kept his hair short or it would have looked like a bird's nest after wearing that hat.

They were all introduced, and Cruikshank led them through to the back of the church, where the office was.

'Grab a pew,' he said. 'As it were.'

There were several chairs lined up for them. Just then, a younger man came in.

'Allow me to introduce my associate minister, Prentice McGuire.'

'Hello, folks. Nice cup of tea, eh? You'll be wanting to thaw out.'

Bracken wanted to tell the young man that they hadn't hiked here, but he let it slide.

'That would be great,' he said instead.

'I just wanted you to see what the church's office looks like,' Cruikshank said. 'Allow me to take you through to the Sunday school classroom instead. It's a bit bigger. Prentice, would you mind bringing the tea through there, please?'

'Not at all. My pleasure.'

They filed back out and over to the Sunday school on the other side of the church.

'In here. That's better. We can grab a seat, have a nice cuppa and get to know each other better. Then Ailsa and I can have a little chat while Prentice shows the rest of you around.'

'Excellent,' Ailsa said.

'This is a nice place you have here,' Meyer said.

'Thank you. I built it myself.' Cruikshank grinned.

Meyer was silent for a second and then he laughed. 'A minister with a sense of humour. I like it. You'll be in good hands here, Ailsa. I hope you have many good years here.'

And in that moment, Bracken knew. If ever he had been in any doubt, then all doubt vanished in that second.

'How did you know she's coming here after her release?' Bracken asked Meyer.

'I just assumed when we got here.'

'Nobody mentioned that. This was just a church she was going to for her day release.'

'I don't know what you want me to say.'

'Robert knew. He had notes in a file on it. He had been told not to talk about it, for security reasons. Nobody knew but me, Superintendent Page, Robert and Ailsa. And the justice minister too, of course. Not you, even though you're the director. The location had to be kept tight, yet you just wished her many good years here. Like you knew she was coming here.'

'Oh, come on, Bracken. What is this? I made an off-the-cuff remark.'

'No, you didn't.'

'No, he didn't,' Peter Fisher said, coming into the small classroom. He strode across to Ailsa and yanked her to her feet and put an arm around her neck, holding a knife to it.

'I was wondering when you were going to show yourself, Peter,' Bracken said.

'Now you know.'

Meyer stood up and walked up to Fisher. 'Put the bloody knife away. You might hurt her.'

Fisher looked at him for a second, as if he was going to argue, but he relented and stepped away. Still, he kept the knife out. 'Just in case they try to be heroes,' he said.

'What's going on, Fritz?' Ailsa said as he grabbed hold of her arm.

'Those bumbling idiots blew the whole plan before Christmas when they had you in that other church,' Meyer said. 'They were supposed to get away with you and Robert. Then Robert would have been taken care of. You would have been mine then, Ailsa. That...I don't even know how to describe him...that *animal* would have been taken care of too. It would have been you and me. You wouldn't have come to any harm, I promise you. Those who wanted you dead would have been taken care of.'

'What are you talking about?'

'I love you, Ailsa. I've loved you since I met you years ago. I knew this day would come, when you would be free and we could be together. But you married Robert. You could have married me instead.'

'Did you kill William Watkins and Kate Lamb?' Bracken asked.

'That was me,' Fisher said. 'It was all part of the

plan to have you hunt them, but then Fritz came up with the idea of killing them and putting them in the Land Rover so Robert couldn't come here today and Fritz would.'

'You were the one who bought the Land Rover from Maxine Graham, the nurse, weren't you?' Kara asked.

'That's right. I was the one who tried to kill you in your house by burning it to the ground. I had already sold the Land Rover to the orderly, but it was sitting in the hospital car park, still registered to Ethan Hawk.'

'Why did you kill your own daughter and the others?' Bracken asked Fisher.

'*Step*daughter. She was such a spoiled little bitch. Meghan knew I was driving the car that night. The night of the crash. I was fine because I was the one who had a seat belt on. All those young people with their it-won't-happen-to-me attitude. Yes, I was drunk. Not falling all over the place but enough to fail a breathalyser. And that stupid woman pulled across the road in front of me and I hit her. Meghan was knocked out cold. I knew my life would be over. All the others in the crash were injured. I got out, pulled Meghan across the front seat and adjusted the seat. It was two o'clock in the morning, so there was no traffic. Then I sat in the passenger seat and waited for the emergency services to arrive.'

'How were you driving the car?'

'Meghan called me, believe it or not. She didn't want to drive home. I said I would come out and get her. Taxis were taking ages and the weather wasn't the best. I drove out and parked my car. She drove away from the party and everybody saw her driving with the others in the car. At the bottom of the hill, I took over.'

'Surely everybody knew what you had done?' Kara said.

'Nope. They were out of their skulls. They couldn't remember a thing. Meghan was the only one who remembered, later on. So she blackmailed me to get anything she wanted. Then when she said she was getting married, I was pleased. But then she told me she was having an affair and wouldn't be going through with the wedding. It had already cost us a fortune. I told her I wasn't happy, and she said she would drop me in it. I'd had enough. I know Dr Meyer. We got talking and he offered me a solution. If I would help him in return.'

'And William Watkins and Kate Lamb would be the fall guys. And dead people don't talk,' Bracken said. 'What about your girlfriend? She helped you, didn't she?'

Kara looked at Bracken for a second.

'Fisher was having an affair,' he explained, 'with

Meghan's friend, Elaine. She was there at the hen night and she helped him kill Meghan.'

Fisher laughed. 'Yes, she helped. I almost got caught. That boyfriend of Meghan's, Glen King, came to the nightclub and I thought he had seen me. He hadn't, though, and I managed to get Meghan downstairs to talk to her. And kill her. Elaine had drugged her by then, so she wouldn't have recognised Santa Claus, never mind her stepfather.'

'My dad was at your party on Saturday night,' Bracken said.

'People were drunk. I was mingling. It was easy to leave and then come back. Nobody even knew I was gone. The bar was free, and when there's a free bar, people drink four times as much.'

The door to the classroom burst open and Elaine Norris came in, holding a knife up, and roughly grabbed the associate minister's jacket. Prentice didn't make any sudden moves. Not yet.

'That's why you only had Elaine's phone number when we visited you in your office the other day,' Bracken said. 'Because she's your girlfriend.'

'Very clever,' Elaine answered.

'Did you have to kill Meghan's other friends?' Kara asked.

'Of course,' said Fisher. 'It was the only way. You would think that Watkins and Lamb were out for revenge. The others were just collateral damage. I just needed Meghan dead.'

Bracken smiled. 'You almost got away with it.'

'Not *almost*, Bracken,' Fisher said. 'We have. Elaine and I will leave, never to be heard from again. We can live off the money in my offshore accounts. And Meyer can do whatever it is he wants to do with Ailsa.'

Prentice McGuire, better known as DC Docherty Lennox, grabbed Elaine's knife arm and twisted it, throwing her over his leg.

The minister, better known as DS Tam Gale, grabbed hold of Peter Fisher, but Fisher fought back hard. Gale had to put in a lot of effort, and they crashed into Bracken and Kara. Bracken was about to draw his baton when Gale grabbed Fisher between the legs and squeezed hard.

The man let out a squeal and fell to his knees.

Bracken looked for Ailsa and Meyer, but they were gone.

He ran for the door, Kara right behind him. Out in the church itself, they found Fritz Meyer on his knees. His right arm was out straight, locked by Ailsa's hand, his elbow about to pop.

'Did you think I would have just walked away with you, Fritz? Left Robert for you? Even if he was in prison? You don't know me at all.'

Bracken saw the knife in her left hand. 'Ailsa, put the knife down. He's not worth it.'

'What? Oh, I forgot about that. He grabbed it and was using it against me. I just disarmed him. Here, take it, Sean.' She held it out and Bracken took it. Then Ailsa bent Meyer's arm and put it up his back.

Bracken cuffed him while Gale and Doc brought the other two through and got them on their knees.

Bracken took his phone out and dialled a number. 'Get in here,' he said, then hung up.

DI Jimmy Sullivan came in with Izzie and a group of uniforms.

'Glad to see nobody battered you over the napper with a log this time,' Bracken said to Sullivan.

'Once bitten, sir.'

FORTY-EIGHT

'No more from Danny wanting to come and crash at your place?' Bracken said, taking a handful of popcorn from the bowl on Chaz's lap.

'Nope. His mother called me and told me she got wired into him for bothering me. He went back to London with his tail between his legs. It's just you who can crash on the couch from now on.'

'What about your brother?'

'Oh, yeah. I forgot about Roger. We'll work something out. The nights you stay over, he can't. Simple as that.'

'It still seems strange that I'll be staying over.'

'I won't be staying over here, though.'

The TV was on in the lounge in the guest house. Ed Bracken came in with Max.

'Don't be feeding him any of that stuff. I don't know if dogs can eat popcorn.'

'We won't, Dad. I mean, at least you only feed him the good stuff. Like hot dogs.'

'Nothing wrong with a good hot dog.'

'That's like cannibalism.'

'Oh, for God's sake. Are you trying to put me off them?'

'Grumpy's still mad about Peter Fisher,' Bracken said.

'I am. That bastard could have chopped me up into little pieces. I'm lucky to be alive.'

Bracken sniggered. 'I don't think he was going to feed you to the fishes.'

'You might laugh, son, but I always knew there was something not right about him. His eyes were too close together. Like yours.'

'Sod off.'

'Am I missing all the fun?' Kara said.

'It's not started yet, Kara,' Ed said, getting Max to lie down out of the way.

Bob and Mary came in with two more bowls of popcorn.

'Saturday night with friends. You can't beat it,' Mary said.

Natalie came in with Rory. 'Sit down and be quiet,

son,' she said. He sat on the floor beside Bob, who ruffled his hair.

Bracken squeezed up closer to Chaz. 'Here, sit next to me, Kara.'

'Thanks, Sean.' Kara sat down and he handed her the bowl.

'Everybody ready?' Ed asked.

They were.

'Here we go. *Notting Hill.*'

Bracken sighed with relief. They needed something light to watch. Ed had suggested *Dial M for Murder*, but Bracken had shot that down.

He got enough of that at work.

AFTERWORD

Thank you all again for taking this journey with Sean Bracken. Despite one reviewer saying I must have daddy issues because I have a character interacting with his father, I decided to have Ed Bracken in this book too. I like the old fella.

I would like to thank my advanced readers who are a great bunch. Thank you to Deb as usual, for playing wrangler to our two dogs. The cats look after themselves and their attitude is, he's a writer, big deal. Just bring our lunch.

I would like to thank Ruth, for her help. Also thanks to an officer who gave me some help who shall remain anonymous, but he knows who he is. Also a huge thanks to Steven Gray, a retired firearms unit officer with Police Scotland, who explained about bank robbers and bank robberies and how they are dealt with from a firearms view point. Then I added a little bit of fiction to it. Any mistakes in procedure are mine and not his.

Killearn in Scotland exists, but I've never been there. I'd like to go sometime in the future. It looks a nice place. I might even go to church.

Thanks to all the Carson family for your support. It means a lot.

And to you, the reader, who grabs a hold of the strap hanger and comes along for the ride. Without you, this would all be meaningless.

Before you go, could I ask you to please take a minute to give a review or a rating on Amazon or Goodreads. Each one helps me a lot, and I thank you in advance.

All the best my friends.

John Carson

May 2021

New York

ABOUT THE AUTHOR

John Carson is originally from Edinburgh but now lives with his wife and family in New York State. He shares his house with four cats and two dogs.

website - johncarsonauthor.com
    Facebook - JohnCarsonAuthor
    Twitter - JohnCarsonBooks
    Instagram - JohnCarsonAuthor

www.ingramcontent.com/pod-product-compliance
Lightning Source LLC
Chambersburg PA
CBHW021423150726

47989CB00001B/84